AF417969

Sam Johnson
The Collected Stories
Volume II

Edward J. Herdrich

The character of Sam, and her short stories and novels that will follow, are dedicated with gratitude to the following:

Linda B. – promises to keep

(Lieutenant) Marie Tyse – still travelling to the beat of a different drummer

My daughter, Tatyana Rose – always strong, always smart, ever beautiful

My editor, Niki – yes, she was (almost) always right

And all the women like them who have shown that compassion requires more strength than apathy, that courage is facing your fears, not denying you have any, that anger is an energy that only requires proper direction, and that the beauty that matters shines out from the soul.

The Stories

ISBN:9781661475871

Edward J. Herdrich

If You Can't Trust Your Client

A Samantha Rose Johnson,
Licensed Private Detective, story

"Faster," Andre yelled, a right hook coming at me.

I dropped, pivoted, and tried to sweep his leg. He pivoted faster, blocking my leg, and then landing a solid punch on my left shoulder, knocking me to the ground. He stepped back and let his arms drop, folding his hands in front of him. Break.

"That bad?"

"Sam, it's not good or bad. Your instincts are on target. Have you been doing your core exercises?"

I hesitated for a moment. "Been running and…"

"More core, less running."

"Okay, Dre. More core, less running."

"Good. Remember, you asked me to keep it real. Your cardio's good, you're flexible…you need to be a little tighter, stronger."

"Got it. Thanks, Andre."

I bowed slightly. The MMA gym was not like a normal martial arts dojo in some ways, and practitioners were allowed to practice their separate protocols as long as they respected the gym's overall fight and warrior sensibility. Some people bowed, some people hugged, some people just shook hands. I always felt the whole warrior thing was a bit melodramatic, but I respected the people there, so I kept it to myself.

"I'm out of town next weekend. You want to work with Bob or on your own?"

"Dre," I replied with a wink and a nod. "You know it's not safe to let me spar with these white boys."

Andre was a tall, dark-skinned black man. He'd served with the 5th Special Forces, and, we'd discovered through conversation, he'd actually been part of a team that harassed my team of M.P.s when I was the assistant non-com at a detachment in New Mexico. They'd dropped in, setting off flares in one spot, building a fire in another. All part of their training to see what they could get away with against trained troops. We never caught up to them.

"Best way to keep them on their toes. Bob at least is aware of that, likes to get challenged."

Andre and I joked around about people who hadn't served and how easy that was to tell just by the way they took a defeat. Bob rolled with our joking. He was a year or two younger than me, a policeman, and one of the few guys at the gym without tattoos. He and I had sparred together a few times.

"No disrespect to Bob, he's pretty good, but I think I'll take the time to work with the bag."

"Sounds good. See you in two weeks."

As I left the gym, walking to my apartment, I couldn't help but think about the sloppy roundhouse I'd used on the attorney I'd served a couple months back. I pushed the thought away; dwelling on it served no purpose. My mind switched gears, busy going over what I needed to get done this weekend. Laundry, groceries, and errands were the price I paid for running hard during the week. For now though, a hot bath was in order, maybe a little extra time in the tub to release some tension.

***

Monday came quickly. I'd stopped in the club Saturday night, but it was slow, and I'd left early. Rebecca had been out of town over the weekend and wanted to meet to go over a few things. I'd received a text bright and early from Michael Vincenzo, an Aurora attorney whom I'd done some work for, something about his law partner needing work done. I pulled into the parking lot for Baker Hill.

"Rebecca, you remember that law firm out of Aurora? Vincenzo, Battista, and Mahoney?" I asked, setting my coffee cup down on the table. I picked up my fork and looked at Becca.

"Sure, *Samantha*," she replied.

I took a bite of my omelet and flagged the waitress for more coffee. She nodded and put an index finger up on the hand that was holding the pitcher of water, her other arm supporting a tray heavy with a half dozen breakfasts.

She went on, "I know you did some work for Michael Vincenzo. He represented a couple members of the Kings...murder charges, right? We used to joke around down at the department about Mahoney being allowed in the firm to show there were no hard feelings over the Tammany Hall days."

I chuckled. "Yes, *Becca,* I did some work for Vincenzo, but not the other two. You have the skinny on Battista?"

"The skinny? Really, Sam?"

"Really, Becca," I returned, eyebrows raised, a crooked grin.

She grinned back. "Well, I can tell you Danny— Daniel—Battista has a reputation for being both *old world* in the patriarchal sense and a bit naive. Not sure if he's really naive or just lacks common sense. Grew up on the money side of Riverdale. Might even have greats that were involved with one of the families, but his parents were both doctors. Probably disappointed he became a lawyer. Why?"

"He called. Something about a service on a client who ditched on his bill."

"Must have been quite a bill. Attorneys generally shy away from small claims against skips— bad for business reputation, frowned on by judges."

"Guess I'll find out. So, no warnings about him?"

"Other than he's a flirt and a *man's man*? Not that I've heard."

"Okay. Thanks, *Becca*." I wasn't a hugger, and it'd take a gun to my head to make me say *bff,* but nicknames I could handle. "You have some ideas about the menu?"

"Just two...little things. One of the bartenders we hired for downstairs, Elena? Her mom makes *tamales* for people, been selling them out of the food trucks, too; thought maybe we could bring them in?"

"They're pre-cooked so we just have to warm them and keep them warm, right?"

"Right. And her mom's friend makes *empanadas* for a lot of the food trucks, too."

"If it doesn't change what we're doing for food under the license, go for it. If they're going out to the food trucks, the city has probably already checked them out. What's up with you? Any new St. Bernards or mastiffs?"

"Nope," she replied, drinking the last of her orange juice and taking a bite of her crepes before continuing. "Two mastiffs is enough work when you have three cats and two toddlers. I told you about the baby sharp-shinned we rescued?"

"We?"

"Well, Jason was the one who saw him. Before you ask, no, I didn't let Jason or James try to pick him up."

"Really? No, I didn't hear about this one. Don't they say you should leave baby birds alone and the mother will get them?"

"Meh, they say a lot of things. We looked for the nest and waited a while. No sign of mom."

"So, what, you have it in a cage or...?"

"God, no! Even Brett knows you don't do that. Transported him to the rescue down in St. Charles. They specialize in birds, especially raptors."

I'd met Brett only a few times. He was a high school calculus teacher and seemed to fit the stereotype: quiet with a dry humor and a leaning toward wine. At first I thought of him as the yin to Rebecca's yang, or however that went. Then I found out he also had a penchant for craft beers, which surprised me a little. He even asked Becca to try some of them out in the club. I didn't like beer in general, so I trusted Becca in making that decision.

"Hmm. Raptors. I'll bet the boys were telling everyone at school they rescucd a raptor."

"I'm sure. Your turn, Sam. What's going on with you? Any new men or women in your life? Sam I Am still your go-to?"

"Nothing new in that department."

"Hey, I forgot to tell you that guy came by the club and left his number for you again. You know, tall, dark, well-dressed, and well-spoken?"

I looked at Rebecca, smiling. "You know I'm not into brothers."

"C'mon, Sam. He's cute! And he seems nice. You can't let a few bad apples spoil the whole bushel."

"Gross, would you want to eat a black apple?

Rebecca laughed. "Just think about it, will you? I want you to be happy, Sam."

"Now you sound like my mom, Becca."

"Could be worse...I could sound like your questionable conscience."

"Ouch," I replied, chuckling. "I guess I deserve that. It's just, you know as much as it sounds like a cliché, all the good ones are married. Detective Jordan—married. Dre—married. Corey Booker—married. Lot of players out there, even some that know how to treat a woman—for one night."

"Hmm," Rebecca replied.

I knew the tone of that *hmm* and was not really up for a lengthy discussion on the subject. "Look, if you really want to discuss the psychological underpinnings of my dating patterns some time, or the socio-cultural implications of exclusivity or inclusivity in dating, let's have some Don Julio before we get started, and I'll tell you a few things. Right now, though, I have an attorney client to meet with and a feeling this isn't morning coffee conversation."

I smiled at Rebecca, and she smiled back in resignation. I picked up the check. "Next one's on you, partner."

***

"Who does that?" Daniel Battista asked.

He sat behind his large, oak desk, his hands thrown up in the air. Short, squat, his dark black hair thinning on top, wearing a navy pinstripe suit, he looked like Danny DeVito in *War of the Roses*. I sat in a chair that seemed intentionally short in relation to the desktop. I had to suppress a smile to stay in the conversation.

I wasn't sure if the question was rhetorical. "Apparently this Thomas Russo does. So name, date of birth, and a previous address are all you have that's been verified? Do you have a picture?"

"Previous address in North Aurora. In conversation, he said he lived in DeKalb for a while and said he had something civil in DuPage. Didn't relate though, so we didn't check into it. Our secretary will have a pic on her phone. Standard practice these days."

"Right," I replied, making a mental note that Battista was a bit less efficient than his partner who would at least have determined the nature of the DuPage case. "So, how do you want to bill this, Daniel? You're out a little over $3,500; how much do you want to spend trying to retrieve that? Good money after bad?"

"Michael was right, you are straight to business. I don't expect to recover a dime really, but it's the principle. How much do you think it will cost?"

"It's a locate, starting with someone we know is a skip. Seventy-five to run him through the databases and check the counties. After that it goes hourly, same rate I charge Michael."

"Okay, okay. Can you give me an estimate on the hours?"

"Not with a known skip. Hours could add up quickly depending on how hard he's hiding. I can keep you posted as we go. Can you give me an idea of a budget to work within?"

Daniel leaned back. He squinted his eyes and scratched his chin. Despite his attempt at a tough, thoughtful look, cost was not something he appeared to have to worry about. He sat up, leaned forward, and pounded a clenched fist on his desk.

"I'm not going to let this little shit get away with it. Tell me when you get to a thousand, and we'll see how close you are."

"Yes, sir. Have you done a postal forwarding yet?"

"You said it yourself, he's a skip. Why bother?"

"No stone," I replied and got up from my chair. "I'll have an investigator run the databases this afternoon, do the postal forwardings and counties myself. Touch base with you tomorrow about this same time."

"Oh. Okay...huh, yes," he answered, stumbling at first. "Yes, that's good."

I didn't know what he expected, but clearly it wasn't direct and to the point. It appeared Becca might have been right about him, and in my mind he became Dan the Man.

He stepped from behind his desk and reached his hand out. I took it and wasn't surprised that he shifted his slightly, squeezing lightly and releasing. Yup, Dan the Man.

I walked out to my Rav, got in, and called the office.

"Hey, how'd it go?"

"Diana, this is where technology is taking us: I can't check up on how you're answering the phone because you know it's me calling."

"Djou funny, boss-lady. How was it, Sam? Was he impressed? Is it good work?"

"Nothing dangerous, if that's what you mean. Locate a skip. Going to text you his name and DOB. Run him on all three. Looking for addresses and employment in the last three years. Going to check him in Kane, DeKalb, and Kendall from here. He has something in DuPage, so I'll go there from here. Have to try a postal forwarding in North Aurora. Probably won't make it back in before five. Be sure to set the alarm when you leave. Have a good night."

"You too, Sam. You in early tomorrow?"

"Not sure. Checking in at Tequila tonight."

"Okay. Have a good night."

I put the phone down on the passenger side and reached to the back seat to grab my laptop bag. I flipped it open and signed on. What I didn't tell Daniel was that I could check all the counties except DuPage from my laptop. If anything came up that needed hands-on research, I could hit it in the morning. I always kept copies of things like postal forwardings in my car. The drive time from place to place would probably take longer than the actual work itself.

The only record in Kane was for the DUI Daniel had just rescued him from. Nothing in Kendall. When I put his name into the search bar for DeKalb and clicked, there were interesting results: two felony drug charges and two misdemeanor deceptive practices cases. The drug cases were from three years ago, but the deceptive practices were only six months old. Those would need a drive out to DeKalb. As I pulled out of the firm's parking lot, I was beginning to think DuPage might be a little more interesting than I'd expected.

***

"Good news and bad news, Daniel," I said, sipping my coffee as I sat in the car outside my office the following morning. "Your boy has quite a history, which might lead us somewhere."

"Is that the good news or the bad news?"

"I see why Michael likes working with you," I lied, surprised he'd asked the question. "Both. It means he might be hiding hard, which is bad. But it also means there are more points of contact, more people who could be tricked into telling us something or who could be convinced to cooperate for their own sakes."

"Are you going to be working it today?"

"I'll get some work done on it today but can't say for sure how much. Not to worry, Counselor. If he was going to run far, he would have done it already. That much we'll know in a few days and within your budget."

"Good. Keep me posted."

"I will."

I took another sip of coffee, got out of the car, and walked into the building. Jamie was standing outside his shop, and I wasn't rushing in to work. I walked toward him.

When Jamie saw me, he posed his usual question. "How is my favorite femme fatale?"

"Hey, I'm one of the good guys, remember?"

"Sam, you may be good and good at your job, but we both know men are not safe around you. Women either." Jamie tilted his head and smiled. "And don't pull that resting bitch face with me. I mean, I guess you got to be that way sometimes in business, but…"

"Jamie, you put up with more from men than I'm willing to. I'll give you my mom's number, and you two can wax poetic on forgiveness and compassion together. Anything new and exciting? You've been busy lately. Have time to give me a trim? Maybe Thursday? Something simple."

"Something simple? Boring. Let me braid you again."

"I got nothing going on right now. Braids are for when I'm ready to step out special."

"All right, fine. You see what's happ'nin' in the neighborhood?"

"You mean the urban gardens or the police shootings?"

He smiled wryly. "Always a cynic, huh?"

"We've known each other a couple years now, Jamie. What do you think?"

"Okay, Sam. You get yourself to that office now. That's my next appointment walking in."

Jamie and I'd bonded over news from the south side, our shared old stomping grounds. We were also both part of *the community*, but our perspectives were a little different about what that meant. I was proud to be a part of the LGBT community, but I sometimes bristled at references to my *status* and other buzzwords like *breeders* that seemed to be a requirement of the community. Words like *orientation* instead of *preference* made sense to me, but some of it seemed liked little more than a version of a secret handshake.

As I walked into the office, I caught a whiff of hazelnut. "Diana, you need a favor?"

"Good morning to djou too, boss-lady."

"You got some hazelnut coffee just cuz you were feelin' it?"

"Djou may not believe this, but yeah, just cuz I was feelin' it."

I looked at her for a minute and smiled. "Good night last night?"

"Sometimes, djou know, I hate you, Sam."

We both smiled. "C'mon now, Diana, you think I don't know that already? Going to fill my cup and then meet you in my office."

I poured the fresh coffee into my half-empty Dunkin' cup and walked back to my office. Diana was inside, sitting across from my desk, a set of reports in her hand. We went over what she was able to find out about Daniel's skip, Thomas Russo. He was going to require a lot of groundwork. Databases crisscrossed a lot of useless information. Diana did good work verifying that most of what was contained in the reports was either old or fraudulent. She'd checked the

Recorder of Deeds and similar public access sites online. There was no property in Russo's name. His only relatives appeared to be his parents, but typically parents were not a good source when you were trying to deliver bad news. I was fairly certain the PD had already attempted contact there.

"How are the backgrounds going?"

"I'm a little backed up, Sam. Those serves put me back a little."

"All right. I'll do some work on the backgrounds today and grab a set of the serves for tonight. Tomorrow morning I'm going to drive out to DeKalb on our boy Russo. I've already called the client and updated him."

"Thanks, Sam."

"Gotta take care of my sista, right?"

"Yeah, but why you always gotta call the shiftless shadies my boys? You the one got no fixed boyfriend."

She smiled and winked at me. She'd co-opted my no-fixed address expression, but I figured she was at least half-joking, so I let it go.

The serves came to us as a referral from the attorney I'd worked with when I was in undercover at another agency before I got my own license. That was a little over five years ago, but my boss at that agency didn't like serving papers, and the attorney's usual process server had retired. It was a class action lawsuit, and eighty-five notices needed to be served in four days. Most were in the city.

Working the backgrounds was mostly a process of computer searches. Most employers no longer gave verbal verifications, deferring that part of their human resources responsibilities to companies like The Work Number. Colleges and universities mostly worked the same way, giving records over to a third-party verification company. Diana would have to go to Cook and DuPage counties to check the criminals; the Circuit Court Clerk's records from most of the other counties were online. Occasionally, phone calls were necessary, but even those were simple because the typical human resources department or college had designated people to perform the task. Over the past two years, we had even gotten to know a few of the people at the local colleges, which helped streamline the process.

By the end of the day, the backgrounds were all caught up. Diana and I were both tired, and I was glad I didn't have to check on the club. I planned a route for the serves. Most of them were on the south side, in the 55th and Loomis neighborhood and the Armour Square neighborhood. As we shut down the office, I promised to bring back some Harold's chicken for Diana. Harold's hadn't really changed since 1950, still cooking their chicken in a mix of beef tallow and vegetable oil. Harold's had been able to spread to neighborhoods like Wicker Park after segregation laws had changed, but lots of people still hadn't tried it. My favorite location was 69th and Ashland, but I found one closer to where I'd be, trusting there wouldn't be much difference. Items not on every menu, like catfish, could be sketchy, so I was going to stick with the basic dinner and gizzards.

Diana left before me. I was typing up my last report when the text came through. It was Sam I Am.

Hello Samantha how r u?

"Hello Samantha?" Either he was feeling romantic or something serious was up.

Hi Sam, how are you? How's everything going in the old world?

I have 2 tell you something. Its going 2 change things. I thought about calling, but then thought a text might b better

I stared at the screen for a minute before responding. He'd met someone in Greece. We weren't monogamous, just honest with each other and selective with our choices.

Ok...?

His messages began coming through one after the other.

We have to b just friends. Im getting married in 2 weeks. Ur wonderful but its not enough. I respect u; don't want 2 try 2 change u. I love who u r Sam and u r an amazing lover but Im not getting younger I need someone 2 grow old with me

Sam was ten years older than I. He was healthy and ready to retire in three years. It was true: he was always honest with me and had warned me this day might come. Staring at the screen, there was a part of me that felt texting this was incredibly insensitive bullshit, but there was also a part of me that knew he was right. Texting this was probably best. It cemented the finality in a way that might be cold, but I didn't want disingenuous apologies or dramatics. The text was really all that needed to be said.

I won't pretend I'm not going to miss our nights together and I'm ambivalent about getting the news in a text, but ok. She Greek?

There was a pause before he responded. I wondered if she was there with him.

Yes. She says hi; hopes she can meet u someday. I know u might find this odd but Im honest with her; she considers u a good friend 2 me

I was not going to entertain a response to the suggestion at the moment. Even if I wasn't feeling the need to cry or hit something, I wasn't ready to talk about meeting his wife.

Tell her I said hello. I'm at work, Sam, have to go. Congrats.

Sry Sam n thx

Have a big, fat, Greek wedding. See you when you get back.

I put the phone down and turned my chair to face the window. I bent over, grabbing the window and sliding it open. A cigarette was in order. I wasn't up for walking down to the street though, so I pulled open the window, set my feet on the desk and sat back. My mind bounced back to conversations about relationships with Rebecca. When we'd met she was back on the street after taking two years off to be with Jason and James. She was the arresting officer on a domestic violence case, and Beverly wanted me to talk to her before serving the soon to be ex-husband. She was happily married at the time, something that hadn't seemed to change.

When she was shot on the job, it changed her life and the nature of our relationship. One of the city attorneys was also a client of mine, and she put us together about opening the club. We'd had a lot of conversations, respectfully disagreeing on a few subjects, the necessity of a committed partnership among them.

I looked up at the computer screen and was glad to see that it was time to start driving south. I double-checked everything in the office, set the alarm, and walked out. As I stepped out of the building, I lit a cigarette, inhaling deeply and shutting my eyes for a moment. I let the smoke drift slowly out of my mouth, opening my eyes and watching it float away, dissipating in different directions, moodiness drip-drop melting in the air. I knew what Rebecca would say, but I couldn't help wondering where my single life might take me next.

***

"Good afternoon, Counselor. How are you?" I said as I got into my car in the DeKalb Police Department parking lot the following day.

"Hello, Sam. Were you able to find out much?"

"Well, I know more than yesterday, Dan, but it's still a mixed bag. Your boy has outstanding possession warrants in DeKalb, as well as Deceptive Practices. He's definitely hiding hard."

"So, there's some good news in there?"

"He has co-defendants. One of them, a twenty-year-old living at home with mom, got stuck holding the trick bag."

"So he snitched?"

"Not to the cops. But that's a rebellion and fighting the man thing. Think we can talk to him a little different."

"What's the bill so far?"

"Just tipped five hundred. Probably another six to eight hours—puts it at around twelve-fifty if all goes well."

He hesitated. "Okay, go ahead, but no more than twelve-fifty."

"Sir, yes sir."

"When do you think you'll know?"

"Plan to be on it tomorrow," I answered, scribbling notes on the file cover. "Hoping we can close it up in the next twenty-four."

I really wanted to meet that deadline. The last time I'd spoken with Mom she was getting ready to go down to Memphis with Reggie to record some tracks. It would really do her some good; maybe the down and gritty blues would even pull her out from the woo-woo spiritual clouds. I knew she was entitled to her beliefs, but ignoring her physical health didn't seem to reflect the balance she always talked about. She would be with Reggie recording, and that was a good thought. With the news from Greece, I was thinking I might even take a few days off from the world myself.

"Call me either way when you hit the twelve-fifty."

"Will do," I responded, hitting the red disconnect circle on my phone.

I sat back for a moment, inhaled through my nose deeply, and exhaled slowly out of my mouth. A lot going on. I grabbed a cigarette from the pack on the passenger seat and a lighter. I stepped out of the car, lit the cigarette, and texted Diana. I wanted her to come

with tomorrow and hoped she didn't have any plans.
She was usually up for a little adventure, but her social
life was a bit more regular than mine. I wanted to allow
for the possibility of following up immediately on any
information we were able to get from the young man
living with his mother, which could mean working into
the night. Better to text now, before it got too late.

Diana, I wrote, hesitating for a moment,
wanting the text to read well. *You up for starting the
day tomorrow with some real street work?*

You know I am Sam. What you got?

*You got plans besides work for tomorrow,
anything with Hector?*

Nothing set in stone. ?

*Talk to a co-defendant on one of Russo's cases
out of DeK, see if we can get enuf to track him down,
close it up tomorrow night.*

*Sound serious...like that. Yeah, Hector will be
ok. Might get me closer to that license.*

*Studying for the exam is the only thing that'll
get you closer to that license, but it'll be good
experience. Be happy to see you get the license too - be
happier knowing you're a good detective, licensed or
otherwise.*

Sound good. Normal time in the morning?

10ish. Bring me a dessert coffee from Starbux, chocolate cherry if they have it.

K. Cinnamon roll?

Nah, thx. I'm going to call it a day from here.

Got it. Have a good night.

I typed an in kind response, and put the phone in its holster. It was still early to call it a day, but going to the office and catching up on busy work was not sounding particularly tempting. If I went to the club, Rebecca would be there, and she would have a lot to say about Sam I Am if I let it slip. I knew she always meant well, but I wanted at least a couple days before I talked to anyone about it. Get this case done, then maybe break the news.

***

"Got your *dessert coffee*," Diana said as she walked into the office the following morning. She carried a small bag too, not from Starbucks. "And I stopped by Pastigel, just in case you changed your mind."

The little Mexican bakery was just down the street and one of Diana's favorites. "Thanks, Diana. Going to pass, but I do appreciate it."

"Your loss. Save the other one for later or tomorrow. When did you get in?"

"About a half hour ago; wanted to get everything ready. Going to give you one of these."

I handed her a badge. It was engraved very clearly with Private Detective, but also carried the state seal. I kept them in the office for the rare occasions they might prove useful on an investigation. The truth was, perception can be everything. If I were talking to someone about a runaway or something similar, the badge didn't really mean anything, but it imparted authority and professionalism to the minds of many people.

"Where you been keepin' these, Sam?"

"You know how I feel about them; they're like guns, more trouble than anything else. But I'm not blind to their usefulness, either. Have three of them in my desk."

"Damn, they look real."

"They are real. State allows the seal as long as the engraving says Private Detective. But being real doesn't change our status any."

"Most folks don't know that though, right?"

"*Si.* Even when we tell them, and we will, that we're private detectives, they'll interpolate all that fiction has taught them."

"You tricky, boss-lady."

"Have to know 'bout people...what makes them work with you, what motivates them to talk to you. Clip it on your belt."

"Djou got it. We leavin' right away?"

"That's the plan. You ready?"

Diana nodded, and I picked up the file, shut off the computer, and stood up. She stepped out, and I set the alarm. The address in DeKalb was a forty-five minute drive, and I was calculating an unemployed twenty-year-old would probably just be rolling out of bed. I didn't know why, but something in the file must have made me feel fairly confident mom would be home. I had already put her there, factoring her part in how her son would give us what we wanted.

Until we got close, the conversation was mostly about the club. I'd interviewed a friend and a cousin of Diana's and passed them both to Becca for placement and scheduling. Diversity was one of the strengths of the club, and in a small city like Elgin where the population was diverse, it was a necessary part of the calculation for a successful business, especially on the entertainment side.

As we got closer, Diana and I began going over our approach. She was smart and understood people. I didn't have to explain much, except making sure to emphasize what we needed to say about who we were and what might be the consequences for Billy if he didn't give us any information. The only promise or threat we could use was that we'd speak on his behalf to the appropriate people, and, I explained, we would follow through. Like everything else that made its way around much quicker in the social media age, reneging on what you promised an informant could come back at you. It was another reason we needed to make it clear we weren't promising an outcome, only to talk to people. If nothing else, mom would see the importance in that.

"What if his mom's not home?"

"Then we tell him we'll talk to her. He has to stay right with her, or his life could be more difficult."

I flipped on my turn single, making a left off 64 and onto one of the small streets at the edge of town. The homes were all small ranches, most with attached garages, few with noteworthy decorations or additions.

Every other driveway seemed to have at least one pick-up truck in the driveway, and there appeared to be a lot of Obama-hating, Marine-loving, N.R.A. members in the neighborhood.

"I'ma guess your translation skills won't be necessary this time."

"You know," Diana said, looking around the neighborhood slowly. "I won't be surprised if one of these folks tries to ask my immigration status, badge or no badge."

I glanced at her and chuckled. "Damn, Diana, you're not profilin' now, are you?"

"*Moi? Bondad,* no!"

"Trilingual now?" I asked, both of us laughing as we pulled up to the address. There was a pick-up truck, covered in mud and jacked up on monster tires, in the driveway next to a well-kept Chevrolet Malibu. "My money's on mom driving the Malibu."

"With you on that. Good to see both vehicles here."

"Yes, hopefully it means this won't take long."

We walked up to the front door, watching the sides of the house and listening for sounds that might tell us anything. Hearing mom yell for Billy to get

down here right now was a good indicator of how
Billy's day was going. Got to be grateful when a little
luck makes the perfect timing.

Diana pressed the doorbell. There was no ring
or other sound, no dogs barking. We waited a minute
and tried the doorbell one more time. I was about to
knock, but waited a second to hear what mom was
saying loudly to Billy.

"Work, Billy. I have to be at work in twenty
minutes. Work. You know, a job? You and your friends
might get into less trouble if you tried it some time.
Where is my damn purse, Billy?"

Yes. The perfect moment to knock on the door.
If mom answered the door, it would almost be enough
to make me believe in divine intervention. I opened the
screen door, knocked hard three times on the inner
door, and stepped back. The door was opened by a
woman who looked to be in her late thirties, dishwater
blond hair, probably five foot five and one hundred and
thirty pounds, wearing jeans and a uniform shirt. I
could see the world-weariness in her eyes, and I
would've guessed that if she didn't have the small
silver cross necklace around her neck, she'd be more
likely to have a bottle in her hand. For some people,

faith really did make a difference. She looked at us for a moment, not saying anything.

"Mrs. Watkins? Debbie Watkins?" I asked.

"Yes. Who are you?"

I motioned for Diana to step a little closer, took my badge wallet out of my purse, and placed it on top of the court documents I'd brought.

"My name is Samantha Johnson; I'm a licensed private detective. This is my assistant investigator, Diana."

"Good morning, ma'am."

"I'm guessing it's not anymore," she replied, holding up a finger, then turning away and walking back into the house.

She left the door open though, so I wasn't afraid she was trying to evade us. I looked over at Diana and shrugged. A moment later, Debbie was back, stepping out of the house and closing the inner door slightly. She took a generic brand cigarette from a gold and white package in her hand and flicked the wheel on her lighter two or three times.

"Let me get that," I offered, reaching into my purse for my lighter and taking out a cigarette.

"Thank you," she replied, inhaling deeply, closing her eyes, and then exhaling with a heavy sigh. "Is this about Billy? I got to be at work soon."

"Well, yes and no, ma'am."

"Debbie."

"Okay, Debbie. This is a chance for Billy to help himself. You know his friend Thomas Russo?"

"Only met him once. Shifty dago. This about him?"

"You've got to go, so let me keep it simple," I interjected, holding the papers up so she could see them. "We're looking for Russo. These papers are for him, but he's got other trouble too. Billy was a part of one case. If he can help us find Russo, we can mention it to the Sheriff and the State's Attorney."

She was looking straight into my eyes, and I held the stare.

"Well, I don't know the last time they talked, but Billy will tell you what he knows...I promise you that. I'll go get him, but then I have to go. If he gives you any trouble, you let me know."

"Thanks, Debbie. We will."

***

"Damn, Sam," Diana said, taking a sip from her drink and putting the cup down on the table. "It was looking so good."

"You already checked all his social media, right? Damn. Anything left?"

"Wish I could think of something," Diana said, looking back at the laptop.

The phone number Billy had given us was, he claimed, the only way he knew to get hold of Russo. He said Russo didn't tell either of his co-defendants where he was holed up. Diana had done an excellent job of explaining the facts of life to Billy about cooperating. He'd stuck to his story. Now we were sitting outside Portillo's, eating dinner. We'd tried every database we knew, as well as cross referencing public sites that we knew were not likely to yield results. The phone number was non-published, with an extra security protection. Short of a subpoena, no one was getting the name and address associated with the line. It was almost seven o'clock.

"Diana, how are you feeling?"

"Say what, Sam?" Diana asked, sitting back from the laptop and looking at me, one eyebrow raised.

"You remember that phone work you did when I was down in Corpus?"

"Sure. Saved you, as usual."

I looked at Diana, my head tilted slightly, my face scrunched. "Hmm...well, you did make a big difference. We should try it here."

"No offense, boss-lady, but little man's hiding hard. I'm thinking it's not likely we can trick him up."

"Oh, ye of little faith," I said, smiling and opening the file.

I went over the file with Diana, pointing out Russo's age, divorce at an early age, and the fact he set up in a college town, even though he'd never lived there or gone to college anywhere. He was a player who'd been holed up for at least three months. We both also knew a little about DeKalb from different experiences. It wasn't a sure thing, but one of the lessons I wanted to teach Diana was that, when all else fails, stereotypes exist because they hold an element of truth. No stereotype truly fit any group, but if it was true of seventy-five percent of a group, take the odds your subject is part of that seventy-five percent, especially when it looks like you don't have another option.

"So, what's our line?"

"Your line, Diana, is that you just got back in from New York after graduating from Northern. You used to hang out with Tommy, go to Kings and Queens gyros, drink a little tequila, and oh! how friendly he was all night long after some tequila."

Diana looked at me for a moment, closed her eyes, and lowered and shook her head. "You better nominate me for an Academy Award or something if this works."

"Don't know 'bout that, but maybe get you a Delicio Tropical gift certificate," I replied and reached over, putting my hand on her knee. "You can do this. Sound bubbly and use all those cute little words people do when they're being coy."

"All right, Sam, but I need to walk a couple minutes, get it in my head so I don't get thrown off if he doesn't take it right away."

Diana walked a little bit, and I smoked a little bit. She took the phone and walked away, which I understood. Before and after a call like that, talking it out was good; once you started talking to the subject, you had to stay focused.

Her voice was one notch higher on the scale, she talked faster than I normally heard her talk, and she added something close to a giggle. Diana, giggling? I could her laugh, more than once say *you remember*, and *we sure did,* and then she was quiet for a minute. She walked back and put the phone down on the table in front of me.

"What's worse: that he's so desperate to get laid he gives up his location over the phone to someone he doesn't know, or that he pretends to remember things that never happened? Men."

"You got him?"

"Directions to the house. He's expecting us at eleven. I had to play off the noise in the background that I was still at the airport. He even *remembered* that little thing he used to do right at the end. Talk about a player."

"Damn, Diana. I may just have to give up pretexting altogether, you so good!"

"That's right," Diana said, placing one hand on her hip and pointing at herself with the other. "Time for a raise."

We both broke into laughter. After finishing our drinks, I told Diana we should check in with the local police in the town where Russo was staying. It was in DuPage County, but they could pick him up on the DuPage County Writ and hold him for DeKalb on the warrants. It would help them to raise their statistics and get him out of their community, and it would help us because they would allow us to serve him once they had him in custody.

At five minutes to eleven, we pulled just past the address. There were two heavy duty, immaculate pickup trucks with Russo Cement and Paving information emblazoned on the side. His parents' residence. This time, Thomas would answer the door himself, and wouldn't that be a MasterCard *priceless* picture.

The plain-clothed detectives knocked, and Thomas opened the door. A few minutes later, we were all in his parents' living room while he was being handcuffed. I explained the papers we were serving him and tucked them under his armpit, the officer assuring me, and making it clear to Thomas, the papers would stay with him.

As we were getting ready to leave, Russo's father stepped out from his second-floor bedroom onto the landing. He was wearing a monogrammed, red cloth bathrobe, brushing back his steel-wire salt and pepper hair with his hands and looking over the scene. The officers looked up at him.

"You cops?" he said, shaking his head. "You got your shoes on my rug. You stain my rug, I'm sending your chief the bill."

He turned and walked back into his bedroom, turning off the hallway light. I looked at Diana, and we both looked at the detectives. Everyone was muffling a smile, and we all walked out together.

"That," Diana said, opening up her door, "is a parent who has decided it's time to stop trying."

"Don't you just love a story with a happy ending?" I smiled, getting into the car. "Another warm and fuzzy moment to remember."

As I pulled away, being tired hit me suddenly. Diana seemed tired too. We didn't talk much on the way back, and she asked me to drop her at the house she shared with her sister. It was only a few blocks away, and she preferred to walk in the morning rather than go back to the office. As I pulled away, I couldn't help but think about warm and fuzzy moments. I didn't have much use for them, but with the news from Sam, going back to my apartment alone didn't have much appeal. I was more tired than I thought. Sleep would bring me back.

Edward J. Herdrich
Nature of The Beast
A Samantha Rose Johnson,
Licensed Private Detective, story

After taking a few days off, an uneventful week of backgrounds and serves, and another ambiguous mention from Bruce about something not right with the prosecutions resulting from arrests by the gang task force, I was feeling a little stressed. I still hadn't spoken to anyone about Sam's break-up texts, but then no one had mentioned him, and I wasn't ready to volunteer. Diana and Rebecca, both seriously committed in their relationships, were likely to make it more dramatic than I would. The day had gone smoothly, and a delicious dinner of crawfish etouffee at The Grumpy Goat followed by closing the club on a Friday night seemed like a nice end to the week.

I wasn't particularly looking for companionship when she walked in to Tequila Teqilia, but then it was rare for me to have to look. She walked in, took two steps, and moved out of the doorway. If you weren't used to checking out rooms, you wouldn't have noticed that she was scanning the club. She stood still, her long, tightly curled hair moving only slightly as she turned her head. Her dress, not tight but fitted, was a designer touch of tease but not stand-out slutty and not likely to draw much attention among a crowd that was filled with low-cut everything. It was a typical Friday night at the club, about two hundred fifty people, a fair percentage on the dance floor now that the alcohol and other stimulants were taking affect.

Her walk, the way she carried herself, was a quiet confidence I expected to see more in the big city. She was purposeful in a sea of humanity looking to forget. She smiled politely when she said no to two men seeking her attention as she stepped around the writhing dance floor and was more patient than I would have been with the people who stepped in her path carelessly. She looked maybe five foot four and one hundred thirty tops, but she didn't hesitate to walk a direct path through the crowd. When I saw her sit down at the table in the corner, facing the door and the dance floor, I was even more curious. Maybe it was because when she sat down and crossed her legs, despite not being noticeably tall, her thin, tanned legs, smooth and well-toned without being too muscular, looked so long.

Young Andie MacDowell with a good tan, I thought and smiled. There was nothing provocative in her pose as she sat, legs crossed, but that piqued my curiosity more. It also made me think again of a woman I was more likely to see in a club in Chicago, perhaps a blues or jazz club.

Elgin liked to consider itself the city in the suburbs, and in both good and bad ways it was. Some things had gotten better since Edwards was out of office. Tequila Teqilia might not have gotten a license under the old liquor commission, the three owners being women, two of them people of color. Certain populations remembered the jazz club that was shut down in 2003. Segregation was still a part of the landscape, though less blatant than in Chicago's.

"Niko!" I called to the bartender, taking the last sip of my anejo shot. "I'm off the clock."

"Ten-four, boss," Niko shouted, smiling.

As a mostly silent partner, I didn't let many people know about my ownership in the club, but Niko was one of my best employees. He loved the job, loved the pace and listening to people. He always worked the balcony bar so that he could talk to people without shouting. Like a lot of people, he mistakenly thought all private detectives were ex-cops and used ten-codes. I remembered some of them from the military police but was glad that as a private detective I wasn't surrounded by acronyms and jargon. Finishing law school gave me a great appreciation for the English language and enough familiarity with some Latin to impress prospective attorney clients.

"Good evening," I said, stepping up to her table, bending slightly so that she could hear me and offering my hand. "May I buy you drink?"

"And you are…?" she asked, leaning forward a little.

"I'm Samantha. I noticed you when you walked into the club; you're...not a regular."

She smiled and offered her hand. "Samantha, I'm Jacqueline. Most people call me Jacky. You know the regulars because…?"

"Most people call me Sam, Jacky," I answered, taking her hand firmly but shaking gently. "I know the regulars because I have an interest in the club. Now, let me ask what I can get you?"

She sat back in her chair, one hand touching her cheek, and looked directly into my eyes. "Hmm...Don Julio...Real."

Don Julio Real, and she knew how to pronounce it correctly. "So, I already know you have excellent taste in tequila."

"Being a cheap date is really no way to go through life," she responded, her expression bland for a moment and then replaced with a slight grin and thin laughter.

"Not nearly as much fun that way. Neat?"

"Is there any other way to properly enjoy something so warm, complex, and sensuous?"

Her directness, looking straight into my eyes, and her slight smile made what could have been a bad pick-up line sound more like a shared interest, possibly a promise. But I knew better than to accept that at face value.

"You ever think about writing their ad copy?"

"I might," she replied, smiling. "It's one of the things I do."

"Really? Perhaps you can tell me about the things you do. You are correct: warm, complex, and sensuous is a good description...Real is served only at the upstairs bar though. After you."

She told me about being a sometimes-writer. Freelance seemed to be the way most writers and even journalists earned their living. A Creative Writing and Business major at U.I.C., she had grown up in Covington, Louisiana. Her family had moved to the

States when she was seven, her father French, her mother Italian. Looking into her dark eyes as she told me about herself, I couldn't help but imagine her at one of the nicer French restaurants down in the Big Easy. Her skin was a tone somewhere between tan and the olive complexion of Mediterranean. Her voice was deep, almost husky, but without any hint of rasp. We sipped the Real, and I told her about growing up on the South side, not providing many details about my life but enough to make it sound personal.

Pauses in the conversation were ended by one or the other of us making a remark about something happening on the first floor. She was a people-watcher too. We laughed quite a bit, and the occasional light touch felt as natural as the conversation.

She got up from her seat, stepping closer and whispering into my ear, "I have to use the ladies' room. Perhaps then we could go somewhere more...comfortable?"

She moved away immediately after asking the question, to me a clear indication she knew the answer. She was wearing Dior, Hypnotic Poison or something similar. The exotic scent suited her well. I couldn't help watching as she walked, noticing the rolling hip-sway of her gait. Natural or exaggerated?

Eyes up, Sam. I smiled, wondering what Diana would say.

I looked at my phone. No messages. It was a little after eleven. I called Niko over and asked him about the numbers. The rush had been between eight and ten, and it was slowing. The club was still close to full, but the numbers exiting were exceeding the numbers entering. Niko didn't need any hand-holding for closing.

Jacky walked back to her chair but didn't sit.

I leaned over and whispered in her ear, "If you don't mind, I'll meet you outside in five...in front of the Elgin Public House, just down the street to the right."

She looked at me and smiled. "The employees...I understand."

***

She grabbed my hand as the door closed, turning to me after she'd flipped the deadbolt. She didn't have to pull me close, as the movement toward her was natural. My hand went to her hip and one of hers went to my shoulder. Our lips met and our bodies touched. The kiss was firm but gentle. A soft taste, a hint.

She stepped back. "Nice. Would you like another drink?"

"Hmm...I guess one more would be nice. What do you have?"

I looked around her borrowed apartment in the soft light. She had only recently arrived in Elgin and was using a friend's apartment in the Elgin Artspace lofts. Her friend was out on a performance art tour, which I still wasn't sure I understood, but neither was I really trying. The furniture was mostly gray, a cloth, left-facing sofa sectional in the center of the room. An entertainment center was against the wall across from it. I wasn't surprised to see both a large screen television and a component stereo system.

"1942?"

"A toast to the founder, perfect. Bag and shoes?"

"Drop them by the entertainment center if you like. Music?"

"Yes please," I answered. "Bathroom?"

"To your left."

I looked at myself in the mirror. I estimated Jacky was ten years younger, but if she had noticed, she didn't seem concerned about our age difference. And whether it was moving to the US at a young age or her experiences trying to make it as a freelancer, she wasn't naive about the world. She knew how to kiss and touch in a way that directly expressed desire without seeming overly aggressive or desperately seeking.

As I stepped back into the main living area, noticing the bedroom off to the left of the bathroom, I recognized the beginnings of Puccini. It was time to relax and enjoy. Warm, complex, and sensuous was the theme of the evening.

Jacky was at the end of the sectional, standing with a snifter in each hand.

How much conversation was really necessary?

I walked over, took a glass, and clinked it against hers, taking a small sip. She leaned over, kissing me, pressing her lips against mine, her free hand moving to my hip, pulling me closer, and I could feel my body reacting. I could sense the liquid she held in her mouth, and our mouths opened up, our tongues touching as the warm tequila passed between us.

After a moment, she pulled back. She motioned for me to sit down. We put our glasses on the glass coffee table, and she sat down next to me. I felt the tip of Jacky's finger trace the length of my arm. A light, warm shiver ran through me, the hairs on my neck standing up. I hadn't felt that kind of reaction in a while.

"You have wonderful skin and...strong arms. But tense, too. Do you get much time to relax with so much work?"

"I work out, run sometimes," I answered, taking another sip and putting my glass down next to hers.

"No, I mean relax. Not redirect the stress, but really settle into comfort for some time."

"I…"

"You don't," she said and stood up, walking over behind me. "Let me help you."

I looked up at her. She smiled. Not a wide smile, but a small, pleasant smile that looked particularly appealing with her Goldilocks lips. Her hands touched lightly just below my ears, her fingers dragging downward ever so slowly. I was expecting a strong massage on my shoulders. This was much more. She continued, using the same motion, the tips of her fingers tracing light lines down my neck, and then spreading out across my shoulders. I was floating...a warm, light wave of motion drifting in darkness infused with gold and yellow tones. I could feel every light touch so completely, my tongue licking the front of my teeth.

I allowed myself to relax another level as her fingers pressed lightly, my breathing becoming slow, deep. Her hands moved down my arms, and I could feel her leaning over me, Hypnotic Poison bringing another dimension to the moment. She whispered *relax* in my ear and kissed my neck firmly but gently. Warm, pleasant, sweet. As her hands moved from my arms to my chest, I inhaled deeply and settled into surrender. Her fingers moved across my breasts, thumbs delicately twirling over my erect nipples. I turned to her, and she reached one hand down to my thigh. Our lips met in a kiss that started as a pressing of lips, and as her fingers moved to unbutton my blouse, our mouths opened, tongues touching, dancing.

She stepped around me, one hand moving to my chest while the other continued to unbutton my blouse. She kneeled in front of me, her kisses now firm on the top of my breasts as she unclipped my bra in a smooth motion. As her tongue and teeth moved to massage my stiff nipples, her hand moved down, pressing gently over me, warmth and wetness starting. Her other hand rubbed across my cheek, a finger brushing my lips. I reached for her head, fingers brushing through her long hair. I could feel her unbuttoning my pants, pulling them down. Sweet intensity washed over me like a warm wave. I let a moan escape, and my body writhed in desire, hips rolling. I wanted more, but I wanted room to move comfortably. I brushed one hand across her cheek, the other touching her shoulder in a motion to let her know I wanted a moment.

"The bedroom," I said.

She looked up at me and smiled. As she moved back and sat up, she took another sip of the tequila. I took one too and watched as she got up, unzipping as she rose. My arms wrapped around her, my lips found her neck, and I pulled her close.

"Warm, complex, and sensuous," she said, her hands now on top of mine, moving them down. We stood there for a moment, my hands pressed against her, feeling her warmth and folds. We swayed gently, and I felt a soft purr escape. I lifted my head, moved my hands, and finished unzipping for her, watching as she slipped her dress off, continuing to the bedroom.

"Yes," I whispered, and followed.

***

"I don't know, Sam," she said, sitting on the edge of the bed, looking at her phone. "I mean...we don't...you don't really know me that well. I can't...I shouldn't really be talking to you about my problems."

"Jacky," I replied, sitting up and rubbing her back. "I'm not promising to be some kind of superwoman, but you can tell me. I mean, it's not so much to listen."

I felt the deep sigh in the rise of her shoulders, and although she tried to hide it by exhaling slowly through her nose, its heaviness was unmistakable. She had awoken before me and apparently assumed she could slip out of bed without me noticing. I had watched her pace for a moment before clearing my throat. Her attempt at a smile as she turned around didn't fool me.

"I got myself into this mess, Sam, and I don't know if you even could help."

I smiled, leaning over and kissing her shoulder. "Tell me. You might be surprised."

"It's...it's a little embarrassing, too. Should've known better...should've...should've listened to my instincts."

She closed her eyes and swallowed, welled-up emotion clear in the hard swallow and inhalation afterwards. I moved a little closer, placing a hand on top of her loosely balled up hand. I felt her initial reaction of steeling herself against comfort, but then her hand relaxed, the fingers flattening out over her thigh.

I listened as she told me about the couple she was worried had stolen her car. She hadn't reported it as stolen yet; she believed she needed to wait a few days to report it because she had allowed them to borrow it for the previous weekend. She'd met them professionally; both were French, and Jacky, like many people, allowed their shared heritage to drop her guard a notch. She hadn't heard from them Monday or Tuesday, which is when Jacky got worried and spoke to another shared acquaintance. That woman told Jacky she'd heard rumors about the couple dealing in fake IDs and other things.

"No offense, but you only knew them a month, and you loaned them your car for a weekend?" I said, not really expecting a response.

"Sam, I know," she replied, her shoulders slumping, her eyes diverted.

I reached over and rubbed her back. Her shoulders moved a little, shifting in a positive, welcoming response. My peripheral caught her eyes closing and her chin lifting slightly. I felt my excitement and pushed it back. Another time...hopefully in the evening.

"Look, Jacky, you said something about fake IDs. What kind?"

"Driver's licenses, state IDs...even green cards, I think."

"Pretty serious."

"Yes, that's why I'm worried, and...why I didn't want to call the police. If it's true, and the police are looking for them, they'll probably go far away, right?"

I offered her the best smile I could. Stealing a car, drawing attention to yourself, didn't make much sense when you were in that kind of business. But then, from what Jacky said, they seemed more like gypsies, and gypsies did not often operate under anything like what would be considered logic. By my definition, gypsies were people who existed simply to thumb their nose at the system. They would lose thousands of dollars as quickly as they had scammed it. That was all just part of the game, seeing what they could get away with, not really caring about having anything permanently. Normal criminals with a long-term plan and motive would act a certain way; gypsies acted in the moment.

"Gypsies are not that predictable; they even enjoy a little bit of the chase," I said, trying to sound reassuring.

"Gypsies? Why do you say gypsies? They were both French," she replied, her head tilted as she turned to look at me.

"When I say gypsies, I'm just referring to a pattern of behavior by certain criminal elements, not a certain race or nationality. We won't notify the police yet, but I wouldn't be surprised if we did, and it didn't have any effect on whatever they're up to."

"What can we do then?"

"What *I* can do," I said firmly, kissing her shoulder, "is go to the office and run some reports through the databases, see what we can find out about them before we decide about contacting the police. If they're seriously into the fake ID business, we'll want to have the police working this, too."

"Reports through databases? What will they tell us?" Jacky asked, taking my hand and pulling slightly, indicating she wanted me next to her on the bed. She placed one arm over my thighs, one hand on my shoulder, and looked deeply into my eyes, her face clearly reflecting her swirling emotions—guilt, shame, fear, hope.

"There will be a lot. I'll have to ask you to clarify some of what's in them as best you can. I'll scan through them and pull the important, useful information. Need you to write down their names and anything else you remember them mentioning about themselves. Guess at their ages if they didn't tell you."

I took her hand, squeezed it gently, and got up off the bed. Talking more wouldn't get anything done, and her mixed emotions would not direct corrective action. I walked out to the living room and got a pen and notepad out of my purse. Paper was still easier to disappear than something stored on a phone.

"Write down what you can remember for me, Jacky. I'm going to take a quick shower."

She nodded and took the pen and paper. I walked to the bathroom and was glad to see a hamper and a linen closet in plain view. I took one towel and placed it on the toilet seat, sliding the shower curtain back. Fruit scented soap was not exactly my style, but it was better than what most men counted as soap. I soaped and rinsed off military style.

"Kind of embarrassing," I said as I walked back into the bedroom, toweling myself. "But can you spare a pair of underwear? Briefs over thongs if I have a choice."

She looked up from writing and smiled. "You didn't like my thong?"

"Honey," I said, walking over to her and giving her a quick kiss. "I thought they were delicious on you. But they're not my style."

"Hmm," she replied, squinting, a grin starting at the corners of her mouth. "Briefs are your style?"

"Either that or commando. Don't have clean clothes here, though. Not sure how long this will take. I'll text you when I'm done. Depending on the time, maybe bring dinner back with me."

"Do you enjoy wine, Sam?"

"Honestly? I lean sweet and white, and of course champagne is always a nice break."

"Champagne...hmm," Jacky replied and got up off the bed, handing me the notepad and walking over to a large bag on the floor near the closet door. "My turn to shower. I may have to run out to the store, but otherwise I'll be here waiting to help you with the reports."

I looked at her notes. "St. Clair?"

"Yes. Yvonne and Guy. Why?"

"Tip from a private detective: if their last name starts with saint, they're usually anything but."

"Really?"

"Experience has proven," I said, a nod and a smile. I picked my phone up off the dresser. "Damn, we slept in. Ten-thirty already. I'm going to grab food on the way to the office."

She handed me a pair of black panties, and then slapped my ass, blew me a kiss, and walked toward the bathroom. The hip-sway was natural.

***

I looked down at the reports and then over at Jacky's notes. She had been close on their ages. No real property in either of their names. Two addresses showed up, both just off Lawrence on the north side of the city. Neither of them had social media accounts under the given names. It all added a little more to the likelihood the names were temporary: stay with the name for a year or two, depending on how long the operation lasted.

It was five-thirty. The reports still needed to be read through a little more, but I was hungry and wanted some food, too. Is it bad when you smile at your own bad jokes? I could bring the reports to Jacky's; giving them to a client was what got you in trouble. We could go over them, and I'd bring them back to the office and create a file. I shut down the computer and picked up the files. What to do about dinner? I texted Jacky.

Closing up...food?

Good Italian close?

Yes. Seafood? Shellfish?

Mmmm

Dinner in an hour

As I set the alarm, I imagined feeding Jacky one of the jumbo shrimp from Cafe Roma's shrimp arrabiata and couldn't help wonder why Jacky had asked about wine. I was already thinking it would be okay if we didn't get to the reports until tomorrow morning. As I stepped out of the building, I took a cigarette out of my purse, lit it, and stood for a minute. Was mom still down in Memphis? She hadn't called, so I thought maybe I should call her...tomorrow.

I called in the order to Cafe Roma and finished the cigarette before getting into the car. It didn't always work, but I tried to keep smoking in the vehicle to a minimum. Generally, I was good if the drive was an hour or less. I looked at the setting sun over the river. The bright orange rimmed with light pink that seemed purple at the edge was nice. If I didn't have to get the food, I probably would have walked home.

As I walked up to the door, it opened, and Jacky smiled. She stood half-hidden by the door, one bare leg showing, in a white poet's shirt with lace ruffles at the neckline and sleeves. I walked in, noticed a light, pleasant odor of vanilla and cherry, and looked to the coffee table where two candles were burning.

"I was thinking," Jacky said, closing the door with one hand, the other taking the food. "Perhaps tonight we could just relax. Go over the reports tomorrow."

I stepped up behind her as she placed the bag on the counter, my hands on her hips, and kissed her neck. I pulled her closer, and her hand reached back, fingers brushing through my hair, pulling my head toward her a little. The kiss turned into nibbling as she pulled my hand around to her breast. I could feel her pushing her pelvis back against me; she moaned lightly and then giggled.

"But, Sam, we should eat. We may need our strength."

"You, Jacky, are dangerous—in all the right ways," I replied, kissing her shoulder and slapping her ass. "I'll leave these here. Make sure nothing gets spilled on them."

I placed the file with the reports on the counter closest to the door. When I turned to look at her, she was dishing out the food. There were two wine glasses, but no sign of a bottle.

"Were they very good? Did they give you much good information?"

"Wha...oh, the reports. Yes, they did give us some good information to work with. There were a couple of records I wanted to…"

She placed a finger on my lips. "Tomorrow, my sexy detective...plenty of time tomorrow."

I wasn't going to argue. As she closed up the lids on the trays, I took the plates over to the small table. I was about to turn around and ask about the wine when she offered me the bottle and then sat at the table with the two glasses.

"Would you do the honors please, Sam? I'm never good with that."

I smiled, looking at the bottle. Jaume Serra Cristalino Cava. I was hoping Jacky knew as much about wine as she did tequila because I didn't recognize the name at all. I twisted the wire, removed the foil, and then slowly pushed the cork up. It popped with a wisp of mist. I filled both glasses three-quarters full, placed the bottle at the center of the table, and looked to see Jacky smile her approval. As if she had been reading my mind, she moved her plate and seat next to mine.

"I think a formal dining experience is *not* in order."

"I'll drink to that," I replied, nodding and picking up my glass. We clinked glasses and took a sip. It was delicious. Fruity and a little sweet, but a crisp, brut flavor and sensation. Better than a few of the champagnes I was used to, which tended to be drier, less flavorful.

"Shall we eat?"

Eating slowly slipped into a very sensuous offering. She leaned against me as I picked up a shrimp and lowered it to her lips; her tongue appeared through parted lips first, her mouth opening slowly. We exchanged feeding each other the flat pasta, a mixture of opened mouths with a tongue slowly offered, and then the slight slurp as the noodle was sucked in. Fingers roamed freely, lightly, just the faint touch of butterflies' wings.

We finished our third glass of wine, and Jacky poured the rest into our glasses. She looked at me for a moment, smiled, and then held up a finger in a just-a-moment gesture. I sat back and watched her move to the refrigerator. In the half light, her breasts were obvious through the silky shirt, and I could feel myself getting wet.

"Now, if you would take our glasses to the coffee table by the couch, I'll turn on some music and grab something."

Grab something? I didn't ask as I was already feeling my desire and wanted to let her surprise me. She walked over, picking up her glass and holding it up for a toast. She winked, and we sipped. She stepped over to the stereo and clicked a couple of buttons; the sexy sounds of a saxophone and piano floated across the room. I sat down as she headed into the bathroom and back, placing a large towel on the floor and offering me one.

"Can you trust me and put this on the couch under you?"

I squinted, smiled, and then stood up to put the towel down. "I can do that."

"Good. Now, one more toast. Tonight," she took a sip but didn't swallow. I swallowed and leaned into the kiss she was offering, our lips pressing together fully and holding for a moment before they opened, and the wine passed back and forth, our tongues touching, dancing. With my eyes closed, that moment—the taste of the wine, the scent of the candles, the touch of her hair on my skin—was intense in its absolute separation from thought.

She slowly withdrew her tongue, moving back a little. "Now, let's sit a little and...learn about each other."

I wasn't sure how long the kissing and touching, interrupted occasionally by a sip of wine, went on, but my shirt, bra, and pants were off when Jacky sat back for a moment, looking at me.

"Now, can you relax and keep your hands to yourself?"

"What do you mean?"

"Relax. Enjoy what I'm doing, only touching my head and shoulders. Can you do that?"

"I can try," I replied, knowing how wet I already was and wanting more.

I watched as she reached over and grabbed the bottle of wine. She slipped off the couch, pushing the coffee table back with one hand and pressing against my panties with the other, pushing lightly, slightly separating my folds.

She tugged at the edge of my panties, making it clear she wanted me to remove them. I complied quickly, anxiously, wanting to feel her fingers on me, in me. To my surprise, that didn't happen.

I looked up at her; she held the bottle of wine over my lips and then tipped it, a small stream running down my neck, onto my breasts. She pushed herself between my legs again, crouching and placing the bottle aside. She moved her mouth up to my neck, kissing, nibbling, and sucking the wine from my skin; I lost myself in her intensity until I felt her lips move over my nipples. My fingers grabbed at her hair. I moved my body up toward her.

"Not yet," she whispered, gently pushing me back.

She looked at me and smiled, her tongue running across her upper teeth. She took the bottle again, this time pouring it directly onto my breasts. As her mouth moved downward, her hands moved up onto my breasts; her lips pressed against my folds, her fingers squeezing my nipples as I gasped. I clutched at her back, my fingernails dragging upward to the base of her skull. As I felt her tongue move inside me, I breathed in deeply, and one hand moved to press her mouth into me. Her teeth and tongue massaged my clit, her fingers slipping inside me, and I felt the rush of orgasm more than once.

I couldn't be sure how long she was down there, but when she finally sat back I was halfway to some other plane of existence completely and staring at her intensely.

"My God, I have a whole new appreciation for wine."

"You liked that?"

"Liked? Understatement of the century...damn, you can teach me things. My turn now?"

"Hmm...would you be upset if I said maybe we should continue in the shower? You're kind of sticky in more ways than one."

I looked at her. She was smiling widely. I returned the smile. "Wet kisses sounds good to me."

After emptying our wine glasses, we walked to the bathroom. The shower was another intense encounter, and afterward we ended up in bed, sipping one more glass of wine and enjoying a magnificent sixty-nine before falling quickly and deeply into sleep.

***

My eyes opened quickly. I looked over and knew she was gone before I saw she was gone. At first, I thought perhaps she was in the other room or showering again, but as I became more fully conscious, I knew she was really gone. I got up out of bed, walking quickly to the kitchen. Everything was cleaned up and put away...everything.

The reports were still sitting in the same place. I opened the file and knew right away she had gone through them. The LocatePlus report was not on top, and being a creature of habit, I knew what that meant; she had gone through them. Some private detectives claim they never go home the same way twice in a row, but we all need a degree of habit and predictability to make day to day work. In the age of smart phones, she could easily have walked away with pictures of all the documents, or at least everything that was important to her.

What to do? At this point, no one knew except Jacky—if that really was her name—and me. Was it better to let it go in hopes that whatever was happening between her and the St. Clairs wouldn't end up with investigators trying to figure out who led her to them? Or better to contact the St. Clairs in an effort to do some damage control? Tell just Diana? Diana and Rebecca? The business card could have been printed almost anywhere. The neighbors, I thought, were the best indicator of a direction to take.

An hour later, my phone, a cup of coffee, and a pack of cigarettes in front of me on the table at my place, I knew it was probably best to just let it go completely. I looked at the laptop, thought about opening it and searching for...what? The artist who lived in the apartment was on tour for three months, and the neighbors had seen a few different people use the place. None of them had ever seen Jacky before, nor did the tenant ever talk about having a friend with that name. Here I was, asking myself one of Diana's favorite questions: how far before a reasonable amount of trouble becomes too much?

I couldn't suppress the thought of Sam that came at that moment. Sam was not exciting. He was slow, polite, measured, and gentle in his approach. He was a gentleman who knew his way around a woman's body, knew how to pay attention. He was gone now, and I found myself thinking about the first time he'd hit on me.

"This is the third night in a row you're here late, going over those reports," he'd said, his mild Greek accent adding an old world touch to the cadence of his speech. He'd smiled and filled my coffee cup. He was the host, but he was a good host, refilling coffees or clearing plates. "I think maybe someone should give you a good massage, relieve some of that stress."

I'd smiled and looked at Sam. He was five foot eight, one seventy-five. He was neither cut nor out of shape. He complimented me each time I was in Paul's and not in a way that was obsessive or made me feel uncomfortable—he was simply offering a compliment. He was the night manager, so I'd seen him interact with other women as well as other customers. While I had once seen him do what was necessary with an intoxicated, belligerent customer, overall he was a gentle, respectful man whose smile seemed quite sincere. He was ten years older than me, and as I'd learned later that night, those years taught him about taking care of a woman. He was a slow, attentive lover who always made me feel I was the first consideration. We came up with the running gag of Sam and Sam I Am after too much Ouzo one night, but it had stuck.

I stared at the cup of coffee and cigarettes for a moment, my mind still slowly processing the moment I was stuck in. *Why the hell hadn't any alarms gone off anywhere in my head? Where was that gift Gladys insists I have?* When I'd woken, I'd known she was gone before I'd had any real reason to. It was the same kind of knowing I'd felt more than once with locate investigations.

"Listen to yourself, Sam. What are you saying?" I asked aloud, hoping to bring myself out of the trance-like thought I was wrapped up in. "Subconscious processing, not magic."

I picked up the coffee, grabbing a cigarette from the pack and stepping out onto the balcony. I lit the cigarette and inhaled deeply. Had I allowed my appetite to drown out some signals? I'd had a few other occasions when I'd slept with someone before really knowing them, but nothing like this happened then. She wanted the information in those reports, but this was an elaborate length to go to for it. But if she was running with the same crowds as the St. Clairs, odds were pretty good whatever happened wasn't going to make and front pages. Why me?

Okay, okay. I took another long drag on the cigarette and crushed it out in the ashtray on the balcony table. I knew dwelling on it wasn't going to change anything or make it better. Without losing sight of the mistakes I'd made, without forgetting that I'd let my desires overpower my reason, I needed to do something other than think about it. At the moment, I was glad to hear Koko Taylor telling me my mother was calling. I stepped back in quickly and grabbed my phone off the table.

"Morning, Mom. How are you?"

"Most blessed, Sam. How are you?"

"Other than a little tired, I'm okay, Mom. What's on the agenda today? Are you back? You and Reggie finish cutting all those tracks?"

"It has been a bit since we talked. I got back two weeks ago, my Sam. Guess I was so caught up in planning for the trip to Machu Picchu I forgot to call. Reggie and I did finish all but one track. He wanted to rework the percussion on one I wrote just for you, my Samantha. He's going to text you the file when he's done. It felt really good to do the work in the studio again, to hear it back after the mixing. Anything new for my tough little private detective?"

"That's great, Mom. New? Well, I had an interesting case finding a twenty-four-year-old man who owed more in child support than he makes in a year. Bruce has talked a couple times about something going on with the felony drug possession cases going into Judge Dennison's drug—wait, did you say Machu Picchu? I know you said something about a presentation at the spiritual convention, but what's this about a trip?"

I sat down, grabbing another cigarette from the pack. *Machu Picchu?*

"Finish your sentence about Bruce, and we'll talk about the trip to Machu Picchu."

I recognized the tone immediately. She was clearly-in-charge Mom, and I had no choice but to respect it. I wanted another cup of coffee if we were going to talk, though. Hell, I needed it if I was going to keep my reactions in check.

"Okay, Mom. Look, I'm going to zap my coffee in the microwave. I'm putting you on speaker."

"Well, really, you should try to break from the caffeine, but I know that's not a good conversation...smile, Sam, just kidding."

I pressed the speaker icon and got up, taking my cigarettes with me. I talked to my mom about the couple times Bruce had drawn my attention to headlines in the *Courier* about drug-related felony arrests, gang activities, Judge Dennison, and the appointment of a new prosecutor from Cook County. I took the cup of coffee out of the microwave, walked over to the balcony doors, opened the shades halfway, and slid the door open, leaving the screen closed. I rarely smoked inside the apartment, but when I did, it was with a door or window open.

I sat down at the table, lit a cigarette, and put the phone down on the table next to my laptop. "So for whatever reason, Bruce seems to be talking around something, or maybe hinting at something about the drug court...not really sure. Now, what's this about a trip?"

"Somebody has their protective mother voice coming on. I talked to Reggie about it too, and he thinks it's a good idea. Machu Picchu, my Samantha: it's a very relaxing, spiritual journey. I won't be the oldest one going either. There're two women in their nineties going, and you know Gladys is two years older than I am."

"The journey is the part I worry about, Mom. Did you talk to your doctor about it? What's involved in this *journey*?"

I searched Machu Picchu as my mom started telling me all the things she wanted me to know about the trip. I found information about the kinds of trips people took there. There were several pictures of tall, old temples with intimidating steps. Reading through, it was very clear that people in excellent health found the multi-story, extremely steep temple steps a challenge. I knew she wasn't going to be trying to walk up them.

"What did you say about the temple, Mom?" I asked, dragging on my cigarette, placing it in the ashtray, and exhaling as I reached for my coffee cup.

"It's really the most important part of the trip, Sam. People who go up the temples have reported all kind of healing effects."

I spit coffee across the table. "Say that again, Mom. Healing effects?"

"Samantha Rose Johnson. I understand your cynicism about a lot of things, and even if I don't respect it, I respect you. Your father used to talk about how cynical he was before I met him."

"Look, Mom, we can talk about this rationally, but don't bring him into this."

"My little girl, if you only knew."

"I'm not a little girl anymore, Mom."

"No, you're not. And sometimes you're not the woman I thought I knew. I'm going on the journey, and I'm going to do what spirit calls me to when I'm there—walking the steps, dancing in the temple...whatever spirit calls me to."

"Mom, I try to respect all this woo-woo stuff, but this is..."

"Stop right there, Samantha."

"You're right. I'll stop, I'll listen. As long as you'll talk to your doctor about it."

"I don't mind telling my doctor I'm going, but that will be what I'm doing—telling my doctor I'm going."

"Mom, this isn't somewhere with an ambulance available within a few minutes."

"Samantha, I love you, but I'm going. Already paid for the trip, picked my window seat. Gladys and I have even bought special leather journals for writing while we're there. Fasting is part of it, too."

"Damn it, Mom!" I shouted, and punched the red disconnect circle on the phone, hitting it hard enough that the phone popped up and skittered across the table. Fasting and climbing steps that might give a thirty year old a heart attack? Great fucking combination. I stood up too quickly, knocking the chair backward, unable to catch it before it tipped over.

I knew the conversation wasn't over, but I couldn't keep talking about it calmly and rationally at the moment. My hand was shaking, and I needed to get some food, water, and juice into my body. This conversation was not going to go anywhere until I did that and, I knew, until I had a few days' distance from my night with Jacky. I crushed my cigarette out in the ashtray and went to the fridge. I poured myself a tall glass of orange juice, grabbed my cigarettes, and opened the patio door.

"Hello, sunshine," I said, lifting my glass and my middle finger to the sky. "Beautiful morning."

ISBN:9798657743456
Edward J. Herdrich
The Easy Way Out
A Samantha Rose Johnson,
Licensed Private Detective, story
COVER-BY-WINTERGICO

"Willie," I said, looking past the unfamiliar little man standing in front of me and speaking to the large, muscular man sitting on the long, black leather couch. "Could you explain to your antisocial colleague the deleterious effects of his current course of conduct?"

Willie smiled. At six foot two and two hundred eighty pounds, Willie didn't fear many people, but he had played the game long enough to know there were people you gave respect to. He knew if his guard tried too hard to stop me, I could put a serious hurt on him, and the papers would still get served. More importantly though, Willie knew the subpoena I had to serve him was not related to any gang activity that might implicate him and in fact could make his life a little easier as it possibly put some of the competition in lock-up for a while, so he was going to accept it without trouble.

"Marcus, you best let the little lady through or you be wakin' up in the E.R."

Marcus looked at Willie and then back at me. "Really? This little Halle Berry wanna-be? Fancy words, bitch. You know who you messin' with?"

"Little man, you say G.D. I say air assault MP. Knock you on your ass before you can blink—straight up bitch, comma optional," I replied, my eyes staring straight into his, making it clear professional polysyllabic was not my only language.

"Marcus, are you confused? I said let the lady through. This is Samantha, and you best remember her name."

I was tempted to grin but knew this was not the time for gloating. Marcus was likely as unpredictable as a lot of lower level gang members—looking for any reason and opportunity to prove something. Despite what fiction liked to portray, getting into fights regularly was not what made a private detective successful.

"Okay, Willie," I said, handing him the yellow sheet of paper. "Court date is the twenty-third. One o'clock call. Be there at twelve-thirty; Bruce will want to go over what happened the day before with you."

"We're not going to have a chat?"

"Not today, Willie. Places to be."

"Keepin' it real. All right. Tell Bruce he owes me one for this."

"You tell him, Willie—you pro'ly see him 'fore I do."

I couldn't resist as I opened the door to leave. "Halle Berry wanna-be? I'll take that as a compliment. No hard feelings, Marcus."

Sitting in my car outside Willie's ramshackle home on Raymond Street, I wasn't feeling guilty about my little lie as I waited for the phone to be answered.

"Good morning, Sam," Tina's voice answered. "How are you?

"You know, the problem with caller ID is that it eliminates the potential for humorous errors and good gags of questionable taste."

"But it provides the opportunity to avoid persistent calls from men who don't understand saying no for a third time is the polite way of saying fuck off."

"While I admire your penchant for maintaining civility, dignity, and a sense of social decorum, Tina, maybe you just got to learn to say fuck off."

"I'll take it into consideration, Sam. Bruce is in trial. Did you have a message, or you want to call back?"

"If you would, please advise him that effectuation of service of process occurred at the residence address of William Clemmons this morning at approximately nine-thirty."

"Anything else, Sam?"

"Yes, glad you asked. Tell him the statute his buddy is looking for is 725 ILCS 230, Uniform Rendition of Accused Persons Act. And ask him to please send over any Illinois Supreme Court rulings in relation to accountability."

"Glad I grabbed my pen."

"Me too, Tina. Oh, and one side note. You know Bruce better than I do, so you can choose how to present this to him, but basically his buddy the ex-cop is venturing into some of the worst contingency work in the business and is asking to go broke if he wants to try working bounty-hunting in Illinois."

"Right. I'll let him know."

"Thanks, Tina. You have a good day."

"You too, Sam."

Tina was far from naive about the world and could cuss to make a player blush, but somebody had to push just the right button to make her step outside her professional, polite personality. She and I had laughed more than once about her ability to deliver the most courteous fuck you with a smile. Cold girl when she wanted to be.

Bruce hadn't explained to me what was happening with the gang unit in Elgin, or why he was implying a larger investigation might be on-going. I knew the number of subpoenas I was serving in relation to cases that would end up in front of Judge Dennison was increasing, which meant the number of related arrests were increasing as well. A crack-down on drug trafficking was not exactly a novel approach, but the number of instances where gang members were being called upon to testify against gang members was increasing as well. Something changing in the power dynamics was the only thought that came to mind, but those changes were typically indicative of larger forces at work. I was hoping Bruce might make what those forces were a little clearer to me.

I looked at the time on my phone. Eleven-twenty. Coffee or breakfast?

It's Thursday, Sam.

Thursday. Lunch with Mom. Apology first on the menu. Though I still was never going to agree the trip to Machu Picchu was a good choice, hanging up on

Mom was not okay. The incident with Jacky had brought out the worst in me and left me pretty raw, but it didn't make my behavior okay. If anything, it made it worse for someone who tried to keep her emotions in check.

Mom's health wasn't good, and anymore it seemed she was on a mission to change my life for me before she passed. She was getting worse about taking her meds, and even taking them wasn't going to reduce her risks without following the diet program. I loved her and knew an apology was in order, yet this lunch with Mom was not something I relished facing.

I texted her, and she was in a mood for Italian. For Mom, that meant Cafe Roma. Elgin was known for excellent Mexican, but not as much for Italian. Mom's life in Chicago had made her familiar with Taylor Street, and she loved Italian food as much as soul food. I enjoyed the menu, the quiet ambiance, and old world style of Cafe Roma—dark wood tables, soft lighting and big booths with high backs. The cliché-ridden marketing of being a *tucked-away little place best described as a hidden gem* annoyed me, but I knew the owners let other people make those kinds of decisions.

***

"Thank you, Nancy," I told the waitress as she placed our dishes on the table. "Looks delicious."

"You ladies need anything else right now?"

"No, dear," Mom replied, placing her hand on Nancy's forearm. "But you know, please do tell them back in the kitchen thank you for getting these made for us."

Mom knew the owner and his wife. She sang at their wedding. So getting items from the dinner menu at lunch was just a matter of a text. Although she'd still lived in Chicago for a while after I moved to Elgin, she was herself anywhere she went: getting to know people easily, calling everyone sweetheart or darling or some other term of affection. She was sincere, but where did she get the energy, especially in the age of white civil rights rallies?

"You know, I'm fairly certain that cream sauce is not really within your dietary guidelines," I said, placing my napkin on my lap.

"You know, Sam, you may be right. But I know the salmon in their salmon *limone* is fresh caught, I know the lemon and other ingredients that went into this are all carefully selected, and I know that food prepared with love is healthy no matter what."

I respectfully bit my tongue. An apology should not start with an argument. Sometimes hearing the same phrases over and over was too much for me, especially when all those cute philosophical expressions didn't change the fact that being one hundred pounds overweight at eighty-three was worse than at a younger age. Circumstances dictated a different course for the conversation at the moment.

"Mom, I know you said not to worry about it, but again, I'm sorry for hanging up on you. It wasn't okay."

"Samantha, really, we don't need to talk about that anymore. Your apology has been accepted. You're right, it wasn't okay, but I know it came from a place of love."

I watched as she nonchalantly turned to her plate, taking a large bite of salmon and pasta. I took my fork in hand and moved around the shrimp *diavolo* in front of me. The sauce their menu described as firecracker was just that and was one of my favorites, but my appetite was not coming forward. As I rolled a piece of shrimp into a couple of noodles, my mother took another large bite. She took a long swallow of lemon-water after finishing the bite, and then looked at me, concern clearly reflected in her expression.

"How was your morning, Sam? Something's on your mind; you're mulling."

"Mulling, hmm? Morning was okay. Served a subpoena on a Gangster Disciple lieutenant, had a little fun with one of his security."

"You know, Sam," Mom said, pausing a moment to take a swallow of lemon water. "I'm glad you have your father's health, his metabolism that keeps you skinny. I'm not so sure I like the fact that you have the same disposition he did when he was your age. You might not have been born if I'd met him at that time in his life."

I paused for a moment, debating the delicacy with which to respond. "So, are you intimating that the father I never met not only contributed to my physical attributes, which I can't argue, but also my personality? Emphasis on *the father I never met*."

She was silent, and I immediately felt a twinge of regret. But only a small one. I placed Mom's penchant for speaking of my father in the same category as her talking about the *gifts* one of her spiritual friends said I possessed—nonsense speak. She liked to revisit subjects, though, and I wanted to be sure she understood I had no desire to hear about him sending money from San Francisco to help when I was growing up, or about the mysterious inheritance I would receive after Mom passed. That sounded like nonsense too. We ate for a little while in silence.

"So, the doctor said I need to switch to a new blood pressure medicine that might cause some heartburn or nausea, and I should be eating rabbit food with the occasional indulgence of something I like...so much fun to talk about."

"Look, I'm sorry, Mom. I don't mean to be rough; it's just something I'd rather not talk about, you know?"

She looked at me with that sad-concerned expression, eyes half closed and smile worried. "Baby, I know it wasn't easy for you growing up biracial in Sangamon in the seventies, especially with me being gone some nights and weekends to sing, but let me at least speak some of my memories. Your father and I were together only briefly, but he was one of the gentlest men I ever knew."

At sixty-six, I bet he was.

I kept the response to myself. Mom was only thirty-one when they'd had their summer of love, as I had come to call it. Whatever else was true of my father, he must have had quite a bit of confidence and some understanding. Mom was friendly and outgoing, but she was far from naive. I was certain that, at thirty-one, she was probably a little less tolerant of inappropriate advances. The appeal of an old, white man from San Francisco to a young, black woman singing in downtown Chicago nightclubs was lost on me years ago, as was my curiosity about it.

"You know you were named after your father."

"Yes, Mom. Samuel-Samantha. Of course, some people might think that was a reflection of being disappointed about having a girl."

Her eyes didn't move away, and she didn't flinch. She took another bite before she continued. I took a bite of the shrimp, spicy marinara and noodles, knowing she would continue when she was ready.

"Of course, I can't deny some people would see it that way, but then neither of us is really guilty of paying particular attention to what others think—for the good and bad of it. I know I never told you this, in part because I was worried about how you would react.

Your father, for almost thirty years, was one of the best private detectives in San Francisco."

I stopped mid-chew, looking directly into her eyes. I was completely at a loss for a thought or feeling. I wouldn't call it shock, unless that was how you described total disbelief and amazement. I wasn't sure if it was the fact itself or that this was the first time I'd heard about it that was more unsettling. I swallowed quickly and gulped some lemon water.

"Say that again, Mom. Tell me again, and then tell me why I'm just hearing this now."

"Oh, Sam."

I knew that expression and what it translated to. She was going to start by telling me why I had no reason to be upset, why it was just some natural thing for her to do. I let the fingernails of my right hand dig into my palm as I clenched my fist tightly, trying to crush the emotion before it spilled toxically over our lunch.

"Something more than *oh Sam* would be good right now, Mom. Anything, really."

"Samantha, please relax a little. And be honest: if you had known, would you be in the same successful place you are right now? Would you have gone down this path you keep telling me feels so right for you?"

"Why and when, Mom? You kept it from me all this time. Why and when did you decide that was a good idea?"

"Sam, I really don't think you want to know the answers to these kinds of questions. You've never accepted anything you can't...what's that expression you like to use? *Verify by at least one credible, reliable, independent source.*"

"Oh God, Mom," I replied, closing my eyes, both hands balled tightly into fists underneath the table. "Okay, Mom. Let's just pretend I might be able to. Tell me."

"In one of his last letters, your father told me about a conversation he had with friend, a gifted empath. He offered it as a suggestion, and I spoke to Gladys about it. I prayed on it, and Gladys took it to her spirit guide. I think it was the combination of your father speaking from that place, as well as the confirmation from Gladys's spirit guide."

She was right. That was absolutely the straw that broke the camel's back.

"Wait, wait. You're telling me you kept this from me based upon some woo-woo spirit guide nonsense!?"

"Just like your father was at this age."

"Damn it, Mom. Stop that!" I said, louder than I wanted to. I looked around the restaurant, and while not all eyes were on us, there was no question we'd grabbed people's attention. "All right, I'm going to grit my teeth and be quieter. So, now you're telling me my so-called father was a cynical private detective at some point, but when he met you he had already turned over some kind of new leaf?"

"Yes, Samantha, that's what I'm telling you. He started using his talents to help people who couldn't really afford it, like you should consider helping your people."

"So, the two of you decided it was better for me to be raised by my single, blues-singing mom? He goes off to his life, sending you money. And this was to make whose life easier? His life was easier. And right now, hearing there's more I didn't know, I've got to wonder if it didn't make your life easier."

"Sam, don't..."

"Oh, yes, I will Mom. Yes, I will. I was the one taking all the hits for the mixed couple having a baby, not him or you. I saw how it worked in the neighborhood; people see you as a victim. Yeah, you had some hard times, but at least you had a choice."

"Sam, let's talk about something else, really. You're going down a dark road. If you just had someone or something in your life to help you balance, someone who could listen to you, help you sort through these things. At least a belief in something more than work and..."

"So," I interjected, not wanting to hear where she was going. "You think jumping to your vision of my ideal relationship is a good place to go? Tell me about what I need to make me happy, instead of asking? That's good, Mom. Real good."

"Do you know what would make you happy?"

"Here's a thought, Mom: maybe I am happy. Maybe I don't need the same things you need to be happy. Maybe all the straws you're grasping for with this spiritual searching are not of any interest to me. And maybe I've seen what your loving relationships do to people."

"Sam, settle down. Try to eat a little. You're always worried about my health, but…"

"Yeah, and what about that, Mom? Machu Picchu? Climbing the temple steps? You're eighty-three, Mom, not forty-three. Christ, I came here thinking to apologize to you, but damn if you don't just push that idea out of my head."

"So you're going to stick with the easy way out?"

"What? What did you just say?"

"Like your father. For forty-five years, he took the easy way out. Cynicism, everything black and white, everything defined by profit and loss, chosen for what it brings in the physical, tangible world. Easier to ignore all the possibilities, just deal with what you can hold in your hand."

"Damn. Guess when I was getting beaten up at recess at school, that was the easy way out. Guess when I was raped at thirteen, that was the easy way out. Being spit on and called all kinds of names by *my people,* as you like to say, was the easy way out. Okay, Mom, I'm done here. I'm done with this lunch. I'm done with this conversation. You take your trip, and when you get back we'll see if we can talk without any more little surprises, without you telling me what I need, without you bringing up my so-called father."

I stood up, grabbed the check, and walked out. I felt bad about it, but I knew it was only going to get worse. She would keep pushing, and I would keep pushing back. She had it all figured out for me, and now she'd decided to tell me the father who abandoned me was a private detective, too. Wasn't that just the perfect icing on the cake? Easy fucking way out. I was smart enough to know I had it better than a lot of people, but if my life was the easy way out, I definitely didn't want any part of the life my mother wanted for me.

I called Diana and told her I was taking the rest of the day off. It was Thursday afternoon, which meant the gym was not an option—all scheduled sparring and classes. Saturday was not far off though. My energy needed to be released, needed to be spent before I could settle down and see it through. A ten-mile run brought me down to the point where I could shift my focus to things that needed to be done at the office and the club.

***

By the time I walked into the office the next morning, knowing my mom was already on her way to the airport with Gladys, I had gotten my focus back.

"Sam," Diana said, drumming her long, extensively detailed nails on the desktop as I walked in. "Bruce just called, and so did that lady attorney whose name I can never remember...B something."

"Diana, my dear," I replied, winking at her as I moved past her desk and toward my office. "Just a thought...write it down." It was a running gag between us—which one of us would forget more things without a list.

I'd met Diana back when she'd applied at the club. I'd interviewed her, finding out she was starting courses at Elgin Community College, planning to get a Criminal Justice degree. Our personalities lined up right away, and after a few months at the club, I asked her about working for me as a secretary. She'd agreed, as long as investigator-in-training was part of it too. Our first running gag was about the sassy, little Hispanic lady and the tough, little black lady who were going to take over the private detective business in Kane County. Diana was five foot two, and I was five foot four, and the field was not exactly wide open to women or people of color.

I called Bruce's office first. Tina answered and switched me right over. "Good afternoon, Counselor. How are you?"

"Except for Tina's occasional *just blame Bruce*," he responded, "rather well."

"You're finding the expression a bit disconcerting then, sir?"

"I know you're smiling, Sam."

Bruce and I, in appearance, defined diametric opposition. He was seventy-six, white-haired, tall, and white, with the weather-worn, leathery skin of a man who grew up on a farm and fought in Vietnam as a marine. Fortunately, our general disposition was about the same. Tina and Diana, who had heard us tossing Latin, case precedents, and military jargon back and forth, were among the few people who were able to understand how we got along so well.

Two weeks previously, I'd been in the office waiting for Tina to get a file I needed for a criminal defense case Bruce wanted me to investigate. After searching her desk and Bruce's, she'd called Bruce. He'd taken the file home with him, forgetting I was due to pick it up. While she was on the phone with him, I'd said loudly "See Tina? Just blame Bruce."

"Air assault MP, sir. Never smile, sir."

"Witty banter aside, I'm never sure if you're saying that *sir* from the Army perspective or the Marine."

"Bruce, never from the Army perspective. I don't know many people who work as hard as you do."

"Very good, then. I need to know what your case load looks like right now, Sam. I'm not trying to be cute, but I don't want to say anything just yet because I'm not sure if I'll wind up with this. If I do, though, I'll need you to be able to put some strong hours in, and not just for a week or two."

"Damn, boss, you sound all kind of serious."

"Look, young troop, I appreciate humor as much as the next non-com, but this is a bit more on the serious side. This one could go at least a year, maybe longer."

"Sorry, Bruce, no disrespect intended. Right now, other than a witness locate for Tim that's wrapping up, I really don't have much in the way of real investigations. Usual number of serves and backgrounds, but Diana's got her skills up there. You really can't give me anything?"

"Call it professional courtesy. I don't want to talk about it until I know, and I don't want to get you started down a road to nowhere."

"Enough said, Bruce."

"I should know within a week; ten days at the most."

"All right, sir. Anything else to report at this time?"

"Negative on that. Not that I want you turning down any work, but I do hope nothing breaks big for you before I get my answer. I really want you on this one, Sam."

"Thank you, Bruce. If it's got you this serious, it sounds like something I'll want to be working on."

"All right, Sam. Time to see what else is on my desk to do. Take care."

I hung up feeling a little better about the day. Whatever Bruce had been hinting about over the past couple of weeks was coming around, and it sounded like more than the usual criminal defense investigation. Maybe I was going to get a break in the Murphy's Law action that seemed to be hanging over me.

"Diana," I said, stepping into the outer office. "Two questions. Did you get a chance to talk to Hippie now that he's back from his honeymoon? And are you ready to start taking a little more responsibility around here?"

"Djes and djes. What's goin' on, Sam?"

"Let's start with Hippie. Did he give you anything good?"

"They had an incredible time down in Cozumel for their honeymoon. All-inclusive kind of place."

I looked at her, my head cocked. "Really?"

"Really." She grinned. "Said he never saw water so crystal blue, white sand beaches and succulent seafood."

"Diana, have I told you about the last couple of weeks? How I really feel like I'm being tested? I really do enjoy your sense of humor, normally..."

"Okay, okay. I know where you're going. Hippie said Jimmy McCormack has been hidin' out down in Tennessee with family friends. Kinda scared. Somethin' about people from Chicago been around lately, enforcers and all that."

"Damn," I replied and sat down in the chair across from Diana's desk. Jimmy McCormack's case was supposed to be simple, but it sounded far from it. How far out were the problems within the G.D.s reaching? "Could he give us any contact information?"

"Sam, who you think trained me? Hippie said Jimmy would talk to us, but only down in Tennessee; he's not willing to come back up to the area. Will only talk to Hippie on the phone, then Hippie relays it."

"All right, all right," I said, my brain trying to wrap itself around a trip to Tennessee. Mom was gone; there was no changing that. I wasn't happy with how I'd reacted, but I didn't regret what I'd said. Tennessee could be a good distraction. I just needed to get his statement and arrange for him to talk to Tim about when he'd be willing to testify. Tim was a good criminal defense attorney; he'd be able to make some motions to delay Jimmy having to come back, maybe even get Jimmy in to speak to the State's Attorney and back out quickly. "I'm going to call Tim. May have to take a trip to Tennessee."

***

I had never heard of Camden, Tennessee, and as I pulled into town I understood why. It may as well have been named Small Southern Town. Walmart was the closest thing to modern you saw driving in. I noticed The Shack and Shand's Fish and Barbecue, making a mental note to ask about them. At seven-thirty in the morning, it looked as if semis, SUVs, and oversized pickup trucks were the only vehicles allowed in town.

When I asked the cashier at the Marathon about the best place to get barbecue, it became obvious that folks down here were serious about their barbecue as an animated discussion erupted amongst the cashier and three other customers.

I got a cup of coffee and pulled my Rav away from the pumps, backing into one of the parking stalls on the side of the building. I took a cigarette from the pack in my purse and walked back behind it. The sun, just making its way over the hills, was behind me, and it felt nice in the morning chill. I lit my cigarette, inhaled deeply, and closed my eyes, stretching backward with my arms extended. I was a half hour early and hoping to clear the clutter in my mind before Jimmy showed up. Tim thought Jimmy's case wasn't directly related to what Bruce was putting me on, but Jimmy's attitude about coming back into the Chicago area was a reflection of the possible ripples or repercussions.

My argument with Mom, Sam getting married, my screw up with Jacky—it was all swirling around in my head on the drive down, and I needed to clear it out. I was still annoyed and a little confused that my mother accused me of taking the easy way out. She knew what I'd been through in life. I worked hard for everything, and just because I couldn't agree with her about her spiritual or relationship perspective, she'd accused me of taking the easy way out.

Do more for *my people*? She wasn't out leading any marches. The majority of criminal defense cases I worked involved people of color. I knew what the system did to people of color, but it wasn't like I could change that with one vote or be some kind of avenging angel. I could only do so much. If Tim or Bruce told me their client, or more often their client's family, was having money trouble, I worked with them as best I could.

"Damn, Mama," I said aloud. "Why did you say that!?"

I put my cigarette out on the asphalt and got another one. I was feeling a nervous energy now, which I couldn't really explain but I thought probably had to do with the drive and everything the last few weeks had brought to me. I lit the cigarette and then took a heavy gulp of coffee. I looked at my phone. Ten more minutes. My feet started tapping the way that Diana's often did. It was anticipatory or...something. I needed to move, so I stepped into the open expanse of grass behind the station and walked down toward the small creek that ran through it.

As I approached the creek, a large bird flew up suddenly, and I almost dropped my coffee. It was a hawk, and I could see the rusty red tail feathers. It was carrying a snake in its talons, and I guessed it didn't want me at the dining table. At first, the wings fluttered, which was what startled me, but as soon as it was in the air, it moved with a bird of prey's ease and smoothness.

"You got a message for me?" I asked the hawk as it leveled off, flying toward a tree across the street.

My mother had taught me that certain Native American people considered hawks and eagles messengers between the spiritual and earth planes, between people and Creator. It wasn't the strangest idea I'd heard from her over her years of spiritual searching, but it seemed like an odd juxtaposition: swift, deadly hunter and messenger from the spiritual realm.

I'd just gotten back to my car when a large, red Chevy pick-up pulled away from the pumps and started driving toward me. A young man leaned out of the passenger window, studying me.

"You Samantha, the detective lady?" he asked as the driver pulled into the spot next to mine.

"You Jimmy McCormack?"

"Yeah. Damn, Hippie was right—be good to meet you at a club or somethin'."

"Yeah, Hippie's funny like that," I responded, hoping deflection would allow the comment to die unaddressed. "I hope we're not talking here?"

"No. Can you follow us? Nothin' funny, just want to be private. If it make you feel any better about followin', my Auntie Steph wanted to meet you. Say she know your mom."

"What's the address?"

"941 Liberty Church Road. Why?"

"Let me FaceTime with your Aunt Stephanie. Then I'll follow you."

Jimmy smirked, but he gave me her number. I walked away and dialed. She picked up right away. She understood my apprehension and walked me around to the front of the house, showing me the address on the house, reassuring me along the way by talking about both Jimmy and my mother. She explained she wasn't really Jimmy's Aunt but was close with his mother and lived just down the road. I wondered if she actually knew my mom, or was like others who knew her through her music and public story. I'd find out soon enough.

"All right. Following you."

"We'll go slow—the streets up in the hills curve quick. Good you got that Rav, too. Road to the house ain't exactly paved nice."

Jimmy wasn't exaggerating about the curves. The hills and trees created blind spots, and a few times I thought I'd lose him or veer off the road. As we drove I couldn't help noticing how many yards were littered with cars on blocks, rusted out sheds, and small ponds filled with scummy water. Dogs ran freely on open stretches of farmland, and almost everyone waved hello, some shouting out their greeting to Jimmy and his cousin. Apparently he was quite popular with the young white boys.

Jimmy had told the truth about the driveway; washed out was the best way to describe it. It had been paved at one point, cement that was now crumbling at various points with ruts that made the winding, wooded drive slower and more backwoods country authentic. As we pulled up to the house that was nestled at least a half mile off the road, I was surprised to see a frame ranch that looked like it might have been picked up and dropped out of the west side of Elgin. I was expecting something a little more run down and double-wide, like many we'd passed on the way.

As we parked, people started to flow out of the house. A young woman that looked Jimmy's age, five children that appeared to range in age from six to twelve, and Stephanie. She looked younger than my mom, maybe in her mid- to late-fifties, perhaps older. Some of it was in her slow walk, her posture, but there was also something about her face—skin that showed no sign of aging, but eyes that reflected both wisdom and worry, inner peace and the work of being peaceful in a world that was anything but. Unlike the others on the crowded porch, she stood relaxed, with a winsome smile, childlike and optimistic. She stood at least five foot nine, and I would have guessed her weight at about one seventy-five. Her hair was braided with multi-colored beads. There was something familiar about her, but I dismissed it simply as her having a familiar kind of look. The others began to rush out to the truck, but she took a seat on the wooden porch swing.

I got out of my car, grabbing my computer satchel with the case file and related paperwork. I had drafted a statement for Jimmy to start with. I grabbed the small camcorder with a tripod. Recording off my phone was possible, but not preferable. I walked toward the truck.

"I'm Bryan," Jimmy's cousin said, extending his hand. "You're about to be overtaken by my children. Good as you look, can't say if it's the girls or boys will want your attention more. And this is my wife, Shantrice. Shantrice, this is Samantha."

"Good to meet you," I said, shaking her hand too.

"Nice to meet you, Samantha. I know you're down here for business with Jimmy, but Bryan and the boys are about to go fishing. I hope you'll stay for dinner—fresh fish, cornbread, and greens. Aunt Steph and Gran will insist, you know. Aunt Steph especially. She been talking all about Ida Mae, I mean your mom, the last two days."

I was used to hearing references to Sister Ida Mae, my mom's old stage name, but not very many people spoke of her as just Ida Mae. Mom didn't often speak of family or friends down south, and my only point of reference was a memory of a bitter argument with someone over the telephone about staying in Chicago. I wasn't sure I was ready for all this. I was here to work.

As we approached the porch, the woman seated there stood up and stepped toward me, her arms opening in a hugging gesture. I opened my arms and allowed the hug but was not very comfortable. I wasn't keen on hugging.

"Samantha Rose, I'm Stephanie," she said as she hugged me a little tighter and then released me, stepping back and putting a hand on my cheek. "Ida Mae's little girl has grown up...angry. The world did not treat you well child, but...we'll talk after dinner. You have work to do, and I know Jimmy wants to join the boys at the river as soon as you're done."

I looked at her, unable to say anything. Part of me wanted to tell her what I thought of her presumption, but another part of me knew it wasn't presumption at all; it was both her own peaceful, self-assured sensibility and something I could not define. Her eyes held me in a way I was not familiar with, and I wasn't sure how to respond. I was used to being challenged or flirted with, but this was completely different. Closer now, I could tell from her thick, wrinkled hands that she was closer to seventy than to fifty-five.

I wanted to deny that my guilt over my last interaction with my mother was part of my reaction as well. I might never forgive her or my father for their decisions, but she'd struggled hard to raise me well. Still, Machu Picchu was crazy. I pushed those thoughts away. There was work to do.

"Jimmy, you okay if we make this a video statement?" I asked as we stepped into the house behind Stephanie.

"Long as they can't see where I'm at."

"Let me hang a bedsheet over the china cabinet. No one will be able to tell where you're at," Stephanie said, stepping away immediately to do so.

"She like that," Jimmy said. "Just takes care of most anything." I was a little unsettled that Jimmy caught the nonplus in my face. She'd taken care of it as if concealing her nephew's whereabouts were any other mundane task.

Jimmy introduced me to Gran, who was in the kitchen washing dishes. Gran looked my mother's age, possibly older; she clearly was both preparing to cook and still cleaning up from breakfast, probably one she'd cooked as well.

"The room's ready," Stephanie announced.

"Thank you," I said, following Jimmy.

Steph disappeared up the stairs to whatever next task was part of her routine. Jimmy explained that her husband was off on a run to Florida, hauling freight for a local manufacturer. With a truck-driving husband, I imagined Stephanie had grown accustomed to running the household most of the time. Living in these backwoods, I thought there must be a shotgun somewhere around the house. I wouldn't be comfortable without that or my forty-five close at hand. Wandering people and actual snakes both required the same remedy.

"So, how we do this?"

I handed Jimmy the draft statement, explaining that he needed to read the beginning of it word for word, but after that he could simply tell the story of what happened, and then I might ask some questions. He nodded. I set up the camcorder and centered Jimmy in front of the sheet so all I could see was a light blue background.

"We're set. You ready?"

"Ready. I just read this part and then tell what happened?"

"That's it," I replied and stepped back, giving him a thumbs up after he got comfortable on the chair and cleared his throat.

"My name is Jimmy T. McCormack, and I am making this statement freely and of my own will, without threat or coercion or promise of monetary or other reward. Today is Thursday, September 7, 2019, and I am at an undisclosed location due to fear for my safety. I am making this statement in the presence of Private Detective Sam...Samantha Johnson. I am aware of and agree to have this statement audio and video recorded. On August 17th, 2018, at around eight p.m., I was present at the Grand Victoria riverboat casino when two men I didn't recognize approached my friend Tra...Steve Jefferson."

I watched and listened as Jimmy spoke about the shooting incident that night. He slipped on names a couple times, starting with street nicknames before giving the person's real name. He hesitated often, trying

to remember details, but it was what I wanted—
authenticity. My follow-up questions were minimal as
Jimmy was fairly descriptive. When I turned off the
camera, he wanted further reassurance that no one
would find out where he was at, and the statement
would not go anywhere for at least two weeks.

"Jimmy, Hippie told you I keep my word,
right?"

"I know that, but it's people from Chicago been
coming in to Elgin. I'm not really affiliated, so it make
it a little more dangerous."

"Any chance you'd be willing to tell me who in
particular you're worried about?"

He sized me up before responding. "Hippie trust
you. You won't be saying you got this from me, right?
Okay, couple people say they saw Freddy Washington
in Elgin a couple nights. He's serious trouble."

"Freddy Washington." I made a mental note of
the name, telling myself I would write it down after
Jimmy left. "Trust me, Jimmy, I know exactly where
you're at. Except for the attorney I work for, no one
will know about the statement for at least two weeks.
Prosecutor will want a chance to talk to you, but we'll

arrange that. And Freddy will stay between you and
me.”

“This goin’ in front of Judge Dennison?”

“No, this is attempted homicide, along with a
couple other charges, but no drug charges.”

I could see the relief in his face when I told him
that and was concerned. Jimmy wasn’t affiliated, but he
was smart enough to know he needed to be down here.
If he was as worried about Judge Dennison as he was
about Chicago G.D. heavy hitters, that was disturbing.
It was particularly disturbing because I could imagine
plot lines from books and movies but nothing I wanted
to consider as a real probability. Movies and books
were exciting but not nearly as messy as reality.

“Okay, Jimmy. I have to play this back and
write it out. I’ll need you to initial the written version in
a few places and sign at the bottom. Go catch some
fish.”

“Do you want some coffee, Samantha?”
Stephanie asked as she stepped past Jimmy.

“Yes, thank you.”

“There’s a small room, the knitting room, just
off the kitchen where you could set up your laptop. I

have a computer with a printer in my room if you need to use it when you're done."

"Thank you. Yes, I will need to."

"Cream and sugar?"

"Black."

"I'll bring it to you."

Could she could tell I wasn't used to any of this? She not only anticipated my needs but seemed ready to take care of not just them but my wants as well. I was moving slowly, but then she didn't know how I normally moved. I grabbed Jimmy's file and scribbled the name Freddy Washington on the front of it.

"You will spend the night, Sam, won't you? Getting back on the road is really not safe after driving ten hours to get here. Dinner will be better than you can get most anywhere. Gran's fish is known around town. If she were a little younger, she might even have her own shack."

She set the coffee down on the table. I looked up at her. I couldn't see anything but pleasantness and warmth in her face. What was it she wanted from me?

"This will probably take me an hour or two, so I agree with you about trying to make the drive right away. I'd be okay the first few hours, but when the sun started going down, I'd have to find a motel. I'll have to head out early though."

"I know. You're busy. But after dinner, can we talk? With a glass of Hennessy?"

"You know, it's disturbing when you do that."

"You're Ida Mae's little girl. She knew how to have a drink, sipping slowly and talking."

"True," I replied, smiling involuntarily. My mother didn't drink much or often, but she did like a glass of Hennessy every once in a while, especially after finishing a project or at the end of a show. I remembered seeing her drunk on only one occasion, and I'd heard it more than seen it. It was shortly after the righteous reverend was moved to a different church, somewhere down in North Carolina. Reggie was over, and I heard her shouting and then crying. Reggie came in to check on me, and I let him believe I was asleep as he rubbed my back. He left after a moment, thinking I was asleep, and it quieted down. "Yes, we can talk a little."

"Well, get to work then."

She left the room, her hand touching my shoulder lightly.

***

As I stepped out onto the front porch, a glass of Hennessy in hand, I felt the dinner start to settle. It had been some time since I'd eaten a meal like that, a meal that settled in warmly, making me want to sit back and enjoy the breeze on a warm night. Mellow was the word that came to mind.

"Come sit by me," Stephanie said, already sitting on the porch swing, patting the spot next to her. "I don't bite."

I looked at her. Her smile was close-mouthed but with a warmth that was reflected in her hazel eyes. Part of me wondered what she was up to, why she was being so nice. I moved over to the swing and sat down, my arms on my thighs, my left hand over my right, touching the soft fabric of the knitted cushion cover.

"Do you mind if we toast your mother?" Stephanie asked.

"No. She's worked hard all her life."

"Good. Then to Ida Mae Johnson, a bright light who shares her soul in song."

I clinked my glass with hers. "I'm still a little confused about how you knew my mother."

"Sam, I know your mother told you about her older brother down in Tennessee."

"Sure. My Uncle Robert. He died when I was eleven."

"Yes, before our engagement became a marriage. He wanted Ida Mae to move down. Most of the family did. It caused a divide. Your mother was determined to give you opportunities you might not find down here; she was certain living in the city would help you grow and learn more. Some of it too, I think, was guilt. I mean she never said she regretted the decision with your father, but I know she struggled hard with it. She worried moving down here would limit your options. Back then, she was probably right."

I looked at her, remembering my mother showing me pictures of the family. I'd seen many different things through my work; I'd once taken a client who had grown up in Chicago and moved to Colorado ten years before she hired me to find her birth mother, who, it turned out, lived one town over in Colorado. The world truly was small, so the idea that Jimmy's mother ran in the same circles as Steph didn't shock me.

I took another sip of the Hennessy, swallowing a little more guilt with it. Stephanie was like other people I'd met who knew my mother. Enamored but…more. Something different. People always spoke of her lovingly, spoke of her grace and humility, and while I could see and appreciate those things about her, she was still my mother, and her decisions had impacted my life from the day I was born.

"Not sure what you mean, back then?" I replied. Technology had closed some gaps when it came to city versus country in terms of personal options, but jobs and opportunity still revolved around most of the same factors. "It's some little things changed, but mostly down south rural is still pretty slow."

"You're right about that, Samantha. Some things in the world only change slow if they're ever going to. We live in a country still tryin' to pretend it's more Christian than most, even though the brand of Christianity bein' sold far from the message brought down…"

"Hell, better than most? Bullshit, plain and simple. People have their blinders on. Heard some fool on NPR the other day being interviewed. He was saying how much better we are than Iran, Korea, and other places with corruption. Only difference here is we make it look pretty—all done in business suits. No cash payments and lots of corporate charity."

"Ida Mae rubbed off on you at least a little, Samantha."

I looked at her for a minute, my head tilted. "Really? That sounds like her?"

"We don't always get to know family well. Sometimes because we make assumptions; sometimes because they shut us out. Sometimes it's too much happened."

"Steph…feel like I should I call you Aunt Stephanie."

"Just Stephanie. Even if we was real family, we're too old for that formality when we're here by ourselves."

"Okay, but then it's Sam. It's some things I hope you don't mind if I ask."

"That's why we're here—to talk, to learn, to grow. Let me ask you something first though, if that's all right? Good. Do you remember a time when you weren't angry? I mean, a period of your life?"

The question caught me off-guard and for a moment sent me back to graduation from Air Assault training. Sergeant Woodman, his BDU shirt off as well as his brown t-shirt, had approached me with much the same question.

"All right, Johnson," he had said, his face moving closer to mine as he offered me the small badge, a helicopter with angelic wings arched around it. "We know you're angry—you picked ABW for your nickname—but can you tell us, your brothers, your team, when was the last time you weren't angry? Angry people don't always make the best decisions."

I held his stare. I had expected something like this. Sergeant Woodman had confronted each of the graduates with this kind of question, calling them out before giving them their badges. I wasn't sure what kind of answer he was looking for, and being called out in front of the team unquestionably required a different response than I might have otherwise given. "When I stepped onto that bird, and when I landed on the jungle floor after sliding off that bird. And maybe when I was kicking Jensen's ass on the rope climb."

"That answer will do for now, Johnson," Sergeant Woodman had replied amidst the hoots and hollers from Jensen and the others. "But when you get out there, remember you're part of a team that needs to know you, know they can rely on you. They need you to have a clear head. So ask yourself, was there a period of time in your life when you weren't angry? You've earned this. It's up to you whether or not you put it on now or later. No shame."

His question delayed my decision about pinning myself for a moment, making me consider that everyone in the squad had called me Angry Sam until I gave myself the Angry Black Woman nickname, ABW Sam. Why not? I had thought. Most black women had enough reason to be angry. At the time, it had felt empowering.

I felt Stephanie's hand on my knee, and the echoes of her question brought me out of my reverie. I looked directly into her eyes, expecting to see...something. There was nothing but honest concern and curiosity.

"I'm sorry, Sam. Have I thrown you off already? I really am just hoping to understand you a little."

I wasn't sure about that remark, but it seemed well-intended. "After what happened in the church with the Pastor, why would my mom keep the stage name Sister Ida Mae?"

"Oh, Sam," Stephanie said, her hand touching mine. "I'm going to guess you've never asked her about this. I know she has a hard time talking about it herself. After the Conference didn't do anything but move Pastor to another church, she made up her mind. She became just Ida Mae, but the record company owned her best-selling songs. Sister Ida Mae was kept alive by the label that was interested only in selling records. That's why she stopped recording for a good while and just played small venues, doing as many covers as her own songs."

She didn't look away or show any other signs of deception. And she was right: I hadn't ever asked Mom. By the time I came out of my place of fear and trauma, I didn't really care. She didn't talk about it though, either. It explained a lot of her spiritual searching, even though she clearly still held to the word of Christ sort of thinking. I took another sip of Hennessy.

"This is a little different, and I'm not sure how…Can you tell me...Can you, you know…It's hard to know what my mother told me about my father and not be…"

"Doubtful. I know, hon, and I don't blame you, especially with everything else you've been through.

What do you want to know? I mean, what is it that's most important to know?"

"Did he really love her? I mean, was it really what she said? Were they really thinking what was best for raising me?"

Stephanie paused, took a sip of Hennessy, and looked at me. "You have a cigarette?"

"Really?"

"When I have a drink, yes. Hardest part of quitting, and truth is I'm a weekend warrior." I recognized the term: some people in a twelve-step program for alcohol or drugs could keep it to where they used only on the weekend when no one from the program would likely have contact.

"Be right back...was craving one myself."

I grabbed the pack I kept in the center console of the Rav—my emergency pack. I didn't want to go into the house and have anyone think we were done having our private discussion. I walked back to the porch, taking a cigarette out for her and one for me. I bent over and lit hers, then sat back down. She dragged deeply, closing her eyes. Then she let the smoke pour slowly out from her mouth and turned to look at me.

"You really ready for this, Sam? Why don't you take another sip of Hennessy and think for a minute."

I nodded, reaching for the Hennessy.

"All right, let's enjoy these cigarettes for a minute, relax in quiet."

I understood what she meant about enjoying the quiet, the taste of the whiskey and the cigarettes mixing, the calm of the night. I never longed for country nights, but I appreciated the chorus of crickets and frogs and the absence of horns, sirens, and shouts.

"All right. You ready? Want you to hold my hand then, child. Hold my hand, close your eyes, and trust me."

I hesitated. I didn't know what to expect. I still wasn't sure why this was important to her, wasn't sure if I really trusted anyone in these matters. Something in her hazel eyes, though, denied suspicion, something that spoke of...innocence. A warmth and calmness that was solid. I grabbed her hand, closing my eyes.

"Thank you, Sam. I know that was hard for you. I know life has been hard for you. Ida Mae told me about the problems at the law firm in college and after you graduated, and I know what came before that. I want you to relax, clear your head of clutter, anxious thoughts, angry thoughts…"

I had no idea how to do that. It sounded like how Dre described his meditations, clearing his mind so that he could get to what was really in there. Banishing anger I understood because it wasn't a productive energy when you wanted quiet. Thinking of what Dre said, I breathed in deeply through my nose and exhaled slowly out through my mouth.

"Good. Ida Mae and your father were more deeply in love than even Robert and I. Your father had been angry and cynical when he was younger, had given up on people, really. Ten years before he met Ida Mae, he had a near-death experience that changed his life and views. He would never talk about it; neither would Ida Mae, out of respect for him. When they met in the city, everything was said through their eyes before they were introduced. Now, don't get me wrong: Ida Mae was not someone to rush into bed just because she was taken by a man. But after a month of your father being with her almost every day—coming to shows, getting her breakfast, bringing her flowers— they made you, child. They were both happy, at first. Now, there are people who would say they made the best decision they could; there are people who will say different. But, I know your mother believed your father, and he never failed in calling, sending money, taking care of you both until he died."

As she spoke, I began to feel more and more removed from the physical reality of where we were sitting. A comfortable darkness, sparkling blue sapphire light, enveloped me. I could hear her voice, but it wasn't coming from a direction; it was floating, omnipresent. Not loud or obtrusive, but more like a gentle wave.

"Sammy, I hope we're right. God knows I hope so," my mother said, her voice appearing before an image of her on the phone. Tears ran down her cheeks.

I could feel the anguish and fear inside her, feel it as if it were a part of my own being. She must have loved him to trust him because she loved me so much that he might be the only person she did trust regarding me. She wanted me to be safe above all else, and if that meant my father went back to San Francisco, that was what had to happen.

"Ida Mae, you know I trust you with this decision. I think you're probably right; people might make it harder if I'm there. Your heart and soul are

beautiful, Ida Mae, and I trust them to make the decision that's best for our little girl."

My father. That was his voice. Strong, steady. There was very little doubt in him. He had seen so much of the world. Two wars, too much politics, and the pettiness of people of all different stripes. But there was something in him, something my mother touched and drew out more.

It was all I could take, hearing their voices and the image of my mother. I swallowed a large lump that gathered in my throat, and as I came to a clear consciousness, realized that my tears had begun flowing. It was too much. I bent my head down and allowed the tears to come. Stephanie reached over and pulled me close to her, rubbing my back in a circular motion, saying "let it be, Sam" in a slow, relaxed manner that was more comforting than commanding.

I don't know how long I cried, but it was the longest I could remember since the time in the church when I was thirteen. This time, though, as I pulled myself together, I wasn't wracked with pain and fear; I wasn't feeling like my world had dropped out from under me. I was definitely feeling a little...weird, a little uncertain, a little unsettled.

"I know it's a lot for you, Sam. Just relax and let it be. Don't try to figure it out all at once because I know that's what you want to do. You want a name for it, a place to put it."

I sat back and looked at her. Nothing changed in her expression. "You really do know, don't you?"

"Let's have another sip of Hennessy. And let me have another one of those cigarettes. They're strong but smoke clean, not rough. Never seen that brand."

"Natural American Spirit. All natural cancer for me," I replied, flashing an exaggerated smile.

"You are bad, Sam. I'ma guess no matter what that sense of humor never going to change."

"Pro'ly," I said, handing her another cigarette and lighting it.

"I'm going to say one more thing about all this, and then I want you to tell me about the most exciting investigation you've ever had, okay?"

"Okay, but you have to tell me what kind of exciting you want to hear. Action, puzzle, or…?"

"Fair enough. I know Ida Mae has told you about your gift, and I know you don't take to that kind of talk. I'm not asking you to change your mind overnight; actually, I wouldn't want you to. Then it could change back just as quick. Just, as time passes and you feel you can, ask yourself what if? When you can. I think that part of you that holds onto anger and pain, that believes in very little, will fight back a bit before that can happen."

"Can you answer a question for me? Just one. Then I'll talk about my most exciting investigation."

"It's been about a year since I spoke with Ida Mae. We usually catch up once or twice a year. It's hard for her. Most of the family stopped talking to her when she chose to stay up in Chicago. It's like I said before, sometimes family can have the hardest hearts to crack."

That wasn't exactly what she'd said before, but I understood the connection to her earlier statement. I wasn't going to ask her how she'd known my question before I asked. I'd taken psychology and sociology classes, met enough people who were gifted listeners to know I probably gave enough clues that she could see that question coming.

"Action or puzzle?"

"Hmm...I'll let you choose, Sam."

"Okay, no complaining then," I said, waving my index finger.

She grinned, and I began to tell her about the trip down to Texas to find Darryl. I wasn't much of a storyteller, but I tried to get the details right and make it at least a little exciting. I gave credit where it was due, explaining that it could have been quite a bit harder without Diana's help. One thing I had learned in the Army—being a good boss meant giving credit where it was due.

"Straight up bitch...comma optional," Stephanie said slowly. "I like it, but I'm not sure exactly what it means."

I laughed. "Yeah, I get that sometimes. It's kind of a law school, grammar play. Without the comma, *bitch* refers to me; with the comma, it refers to them. Really, just like the way it sounds."

"It definitely comes across tough. All right, my little niece, I think it's past my bedtime."

"Auntie Stephanie has an early bedtime?"

"Child, you get to my age and tell me if eleven-thirty sound like an early bedtime when you have to get these kids up for church."

I reached over to the ashtray on the coffee table and crushed my cigarette out. "You're right. I want to be up and gone before the roads start getting busy."

"All right then, Sam. Thank you. Thank you for taking the time and for trusting me. I know that wasn't easy."

"Mostly, easy and I don't talk much," I said, standing up as she did and winking. "Thank you for the Hennessy. And the honesty."

"Give me a hug, child. Then get your skinny butt to bed."

As we walked into the house, I wondered how we'd seemed to bond so quickly. But as I walked up the stairs to the bedroom, my thoughts were about my mother and her insistence on taking a trip that would challenge an in-shape forty-something. As my mind started moving into that cluttered place before sleep, the thought of taking the easy way out rose back up, and I decided sleep was a good idea.

***

After a night of fitful sleep, I woke up a little slow. What had happened last night? How much of it was just the Hennessy? How much of it was Stephanie's ability to see into me, her calm and strength? She'd seemed to be saying it had something to do with this *gift* my mother and Gladys insisted I possessed. That was a lot to accept, no matter who was saying it. As my mind returned to the real reason I was in Tennessee, my energy started picking up. I hopped in the shower, packed up, and went downstairs. Stephanie and Gran were sitting in the kitchen, talking over coffee.

I decided to have a cup of coffee with them. Stephanie smiled and winked, but never spoke of what had happened the night before. We talked about the politics of the day and how little really changed for people of color, especially after so many of Obama's measure were being reeled back in.

I left after having coffee with Stephanie and Gran. Traffic was light, and other than stopping for gas, the drive was uninterrupted. I spoke briefly with Diana and was glad to hear all was going well. I welcomed uneventful days.

It was dark when I parked the car at home, dark and warm. I still had half a cup of coffee from my stop for gas. Coffee and a cigarette would be nice. Take a moment to think about nothing. Lighting the cigarette after taking a sip of coffee, I felt my phone vibrate.

It was a text from Reggie.

Sam, how r u? Sending you the file for Get Out of My Way, what ur mom called Samantha's Song. It's

I opened the attached file.

Started hard on Sangamon
Kids holla colors, sometimes worse
Beat down the diverse
Looked for a man my mama say care
Like a ghost or a whisper, not really there

It's like I heard the Lord say
As if this had to be the way
Lookin in to make it begin
It's like I heard Creator say
Hey you, get out of my way

With the hint of a woman, abuse wandered in
The House of the Lord, worst kind of sin
Uncle Sam seemed a way, maybe help me get
through
But can't be what they say - tainted red, white
and blue
Seem like more I know, the less I see

Who and where in this world I'm supposed to be

It's like I heard the Lord say
As if this had to be the way
Lookin in to make it begin
It's like I heard Spirit say
Hey you, get out of my way

A man want this and a woman want that, thinkin
it through
Give me a break lord, give me a clue
Beyond the noise and the drink, what should I
think
Love got a way in the mirror I just can't see
Need it now and I need it straight
Help me find a way, at least open a gate

Been thinking I should have been prayin
Took so long, now I see what you were sayin
So I look where it is I hold
And say

It's like I heard the Lord say
As if this had to be the way

I read it over twice, not sure what to make of the reference to the Lord, Creator, and Spirit. Creator was about the only one I was comfortable with, but even then I wasn't sure if my mother was writing with me in mind.

It was late, and I was tired. I needed sleep. After a good six to eight hours, I wouldn't have difficulty understanding what the song was saying, and I might be able to recognize what it was about the song that was making me feel melancholy and irritated. But, I thought as I closed the file on my phone's screen, perhaps it was nothing more than recognizing it wasn't often someone wrote a song for you. Or something like that.

The alarm woke me at six-fifteen, and I was ready for a good run. When I got back, I put on coffee and showered quickly. I didn't have to rush to get into the office, so I made myself an omelet with Gouda, onion, and red pepper. As I cooked, I considered the remarks my mother had made about my healthy lifestyle and smoking. Which, of course, made me want to have a cigarette and coffee. After eating.

After breakfast, I was surprised to see it was almost nine already. I called Tim.

"Morning, Tim. I have your statement, audio and video. Can we get the State's Attorney to agree to speak to him without revealing where he's staying?"

"This State's Attorney, we probably can convince her to work with us under the circumstances. And I think Judge McHallahan will allow it. Jimmy's really worried?"

"Even though this wasn't directly gang-related, he's still pretty scared. And Bruce has been talking about something going on with Judge Dennison's drug court."

"Bruce would know, Sam. Get me your invoice. Jimmy's family put money in for you."

I hung up with Tim, finished my cigarette, and crushed it out. For a brief moment, I was tempted to call my mother, but the impulse faded just as quickly when I thought of how that conversation might go. Despite what had happened down in Tennessee, I still didn't understand why she insisted on this trip and was a little disappointed that Reggie had encouraged her to go. I appreciated that he'd sent me the song and did so because he respected my mother's wishes, but it seemed to me a good friend would have advised her against trying to walk the steps of the temple. Maybe she was right, though; maybe we did share the habit of not caring what other people thought.

"Time to get to work, Sam," I said aloud and slipped the phone in its holster. "Time to get to work."

Edward J. Herdrich
The Depths
A Samantha Rose Johnson,
Licensed Private Detective, story
ISBN:9798679965775

The Depths

I took a sip of coffee and turned away from the computer, looking at my wrapped hand. Despite my conversation with Stephanie a week earlier, I'd let my emotion take control at Saturday's workout. I knew better than to go too hard on the bag, but the news of Sam, my argument with my mom before she left, and what had happened with Jacky all came together, and I'd thrown a punch that made contact too hard and at an angle. I'd allowed my emotions too much berth and was paying the price. But, I told myself, at least it wasn't my strong hand.

When I'd gotten in I'd told Diana I wanted a bit of a break, and so far the morning had been quiet. I wanted to deny it, but I was beginning to regret some of the things I'd said to my mom before she left. Or at least the way that I'd said them. Stephanie helped me to realize she'd gone through tough times and made hard choices to take care of me, but no matter what she or Stephanie said, I was still having trouble making peace with or understanding her defending my father. Despite that experience in Tennessee and having a sense my parents really did come to the decision together, it still seemed...odd. It seemed like the rationale was faulty, especially because my mother would say things like two people can always stand stronger together than one when she was talking about my choice to remain uncommitted.

"Sam," Diana called as she walked up to my office door, breaking the thought. I was sort of glad for that. Regret reminded me of sore spots. "You know a woman named Kathy Dunne?"

"Kathy Dunne? Hmm...oh wait, yes. Kathy, Glady's daughter. You know my mom's friend. She called?"

"Yeah. Sounded really upset. Said she needed to talk to you, like right away...somethin' about her son."

"Her son? Damn, he's gotta be at least in his mid-twenties. Well...never know. Give me the number."

Diana handed me a slip of paper. "When you do that, boss-lady?"

I looked at the Ace bandage on my hand and back at Diana. "I'd tell you, but then I'd have to kill you."

"Seem like lately you always a special kind of funny on Monday mornings—hope your man gets back from Greece soon."

I bit my tongue and let her walk back to her desk. I hadn't told Diana or anyone else about the last text I'd gotten from Sam a couple weeks ago. I was still trying to decide if he was a complete asshole for texting the news to me, or if he was respecting the person he knew me to be. He'd said all nice things, and I knew he meant them. But that didn't change the fact he was coming back with a wife, and our relationship would have to change or end. I knew it would have to end because while I would still go to Paul's, still be friendly when I saw him, I'd shift my free time elsewhere. It was the out of the blue that bothered me more than anything else. He'd mentioned feeling like he needed something more a few times lately, but I guess part of me felt it was something that would pass.

"No time for that now," I told myself and dialed the number.

"Hello?"

"Hello, Kathy?"

"Yes, is this Sam?"

"Yes, ma'am. Diana said you sounded upset. What's going on?"

I listened as Kathy told me about her son's health problems and her unreasonably controlling and possessive ex-husband. She told me about the breakdown of their relationship and that she and her son had had a couple of falling outs in the past, due to the manipulation of her ex. She threw in terms like enigma, phrases like spiritually vacant and separated soul. I heard two very different people who grew apart. Her son Ronald had gone down to Florida to be with his father on two occasions, staying only for a couple months and then coming back after he grew weary of alcohol and anger, according to Kathy. Ronald had some form of liver disease and needed regular treatments and medicine, which he hadn't gotten in Florida. Kathy said she hadn't heard from him in three weeks, and that was unusual. She'd tried calling his job, but they had a strict policy of not releasing any information other than that he was on an extended leave of absence. She had driven by his condo and seen his car there, but no one ever answered the door or the phone. She knew the lights could be programmed— anti-burglar protocols for people on vacation.

"You want me to find Ronald if I can? Talk to him, have him call you?"

"Yes. God bless you, Sam, yes. Make sure he's healthy—taking his medicine. Who knows, maybe he's home and just not wanting to talk to me. He broke up with his girlfriend a little while before I stopped hearing from him."

"He give you a reason why?"

"Yes...a little...I mean, I don't really know. Something about her being too controlling. He was upset at the time, couldn't tell if he was angry or...well, you know. Young men who have fathers like Ronald's, they're taught that crying makes them look week."

"I know," I responded, not really concerned about the socio-cultural dynamics of the American male. "I need you to listen to me Kathy, carefully."

"Okay, I'm listening. Just tell me what..."

"No, Kathy, listen," I interjected and paused for a second to be sure she understood. "Ronald is an adult, which means if you're just asking me to find your son because you haven't heard from him, there are a lot of databases and steps I can't take. Now, if you go to the Hoffman Estates police and tell them of your concern because of his health, if you tell me you believe he hasn't had his medicine, well then, that's a different matter. Do you understand?"

"Yes, I understand. I believe he hasn't had his meds and might be in danger and not even aware of it."

"Okay, good. Text me his full name, date of birth, Social if you have it, current and previous addresses. Then, go immediately to Hoffman P.D. I'll get some of the database searching done while you do that. When you call me and tell me you're back, I'll go out on the street."

"Okay. Thank you. How much will this cost? I'm going to pay you, Sam."

"You get the friends and family rate, Kathy. Forty-five an hour, plus expenses, and I won't be watching the clock hard. Is this the first time he's done this?"

"Well...no, not really. He did this a few years ago, too, when his father was trying to convince him to move down to Florida. He cut himself off from all contact."

"A few years ago? Was that close to the divorce?"

"I guess…yes. It was just two years after the divorce. His father tried to turn him against me always."

"Okay, Kathy. We'll get started on it, but even with friends and family, locating adults isn't a guaranteed quick and easy."

"I know you'll find him. My mom says that's part of your gift, part of why your soul chose to come here this way at this time. Thank you, Sam. I'm getting off the phone now, going straight to the police."

"Be sure to tell them how often he needs his meds and treatments."

"I will, yes. Thank you."

"Okay, call me when you get back."

I knew if I didn't hang up there would be at least a few more thank yous and God blesses. The mention of Gladys's reference to my gift had tempted me to hang up. Mom was down in Machu Picchu right now with Gladys, and I was still wishing our last conversation hadn't gone quite so badly. Sometimes the way I said something was as bad as or worse than what I said. I regretted the anger more than the words. Some of what I said may have been unnecessary, but none of it was far from the truth.

"Diana," I said, a finger on the intercom button. "Going to forward you a text. Do a cursory on Google and social media. Start pulling locate reports from all three databases on Ronald, highlight any Florida addresses within the last year. I'm going to run the counties and check the lock-ups—he's still a twenty-four year old male, spiritual influences aside."

"Okay," Diana replied.

Her simple okay told me she was reading my mood correctly. Diana didn't know Gladys or Kathy, but she had heard me speak of Gladys and my mother's spiritual searching once or twice. I didn't mind a serious conversation about the news and politics of the day once in a while, occasionally even a foray into subjects like social justice, but food, tequila, and the work at hand were subjects that were more conducive to a relaxed office atmosphere. I scowled and entered the address for the Kane County Circuit Clerk.

***

"Sam, I got those reports," Diana said, handing them to me. "But you got to call Bruce. I never got a chance to check voicemails earlier. He called last night. Funny, cause he said it was important but not urgent.

Somethin' about that shooting two months ago, the one on Raymond."

"Okay. I'll call him today; he goes on his annual anniversary trip next week. If it's the homicide on Raymond, it might not be urgent because the State only finished charging people...be a while before anyone goes on trial. Let's go over what you found."

Diana showed me the reports on the Dunne case, pointing out the connections to Florida, his employment, and where Ronald's younger brother was living. She had already verified his employment through the service: records as of last payroll showed he was still employed. She had cross-referenced the Florida addresses through the Recorder of Deeds and found two properties were rental units and one belonged to Ronald's father. There were still a couple checks that could be done, but it was very good work.

"Excelente, Diana."

"Gracias, boss-lady," Diana replied, a wide grin stretching the corners of her mouth. "Y, que haras ahora?"

"I'ma guess that's asking what I'm going to do now...got the que and ahora."

"Muy bueno, Sam. You got it. We should talk more Spanish in the office, boss. Keep you learnin'."

"And, while that is true, when you get that license, I'll be directing the Spanish speakers your way. To answer your question, though, I'm going to call Bruce and set that up. Want you to check the lock-ups here, tri-county, and then find and check the lock-ups around the Florida addresses."

"You taught me well, Sam. Already checked here. He's not in Kane, Kendall, DeKalb, or DuPage. Google came back with his Facebook, a couple articles from his high school sports days, and lots of ads for Classmates and Ancestry. That was really all on the first two pages; I didn't go past that because it all looked the same. He hasn't posted on Facebook or Twitter for at least two months, even longer for LinkedIn. People have been tryin' to reach him, but nothing coming back. Should we check Florida? You think he might be down there?"

"Checked DuPage too? You are getting good. Work told mom he's on an extended leave. Could be anywhere, but that's a place we can check at least. Going to call Bruce now."

Tina told me Bruce would be back in a half hour. I told her I would stop by and talk to him. She said that was a good idea; Bruce was "more animated" than she'd seen him in a while. To me, imagining that phrase applying to Bruce's behavior was difficult. I could read the changes in Bruce's facial expressions and movements to see when he was excited about something, but "animated" seemed a stretch. Seventy-three and a marine, he didn't seem to be someone "animated" really applied to.

Diana appeared at my office door. "Not in lock-up anywhere near the addresses in Florida."

"Okay," I responded, picking up my coffee cup and taking a sip. I wanted a cigarette. My fingers tapped on the desktop. "I have to meet with Bruce. Then I'll take a drive by the apartment. Going to take the two wage garnishments with me to serve. You want to pretext the work?"

"Should I call or go there?"

"Which do you think would work best?"

Diana put her hands on her hips, her face scrunched. "Go there, talk to the people at the dock? Play the old girlfriend looking to hook back up?"

I looked at the wide-eyed, pouty-lipped face she added at the end. "Who wouldn't feel sympathy?"

She smiled.

"If we can't turn anything up, maybe we'll dig a little deeper on the net."

***

"This is not like the other cases you've worked for me before, Sam. You understand that? I'm going to have you specially appointed by the court."

"Oh, dear. Playing by all the rules. I'm to be a motion in limine? But will I be an amicus curiae?"

"A friend of the court? Hmm...not sure about that, but I'm glad to have you on our side. Fill out this form for me. You'll be getting paid by the state. Fifty dollars an hour. I know it's less than what you're used to, but whatever hours you document, you'll get paid for—detailed reports."

"You're representing one of the shooters on Raymond?"

"If it were simply that, I'd handle this alone. I'll be working with two other attorneys. Tina will give you their information on your way out. We're working on behalf of the man accused of orchestrating the events, Damion Jackson. Ever met him?"

"No, can't say I've had the pleasure. Willie mentioned him a couple times. You've represented him before?"

"A couple times. Represented his younger brother, too. They call his younger brother Cat Eyes."

"Cat Eyes? Desmond Jackson?"

"Yes, you know Desmond?"

"Did some work for Tim where Desmond was a witness. Damion must be pretty high up in the G.D. hierarchy."

"You know how it works, Sam. High up out here doesn't mean much in Chicago. The Elgin people are still subject to outside orders. That's going to be one of our main points to attempt to show."

"So I fill out the paperwork. Then what?"

"Nothing right away. I have to go before Judge Dennison with this and three other motions. The state has their right to object. Not likely they will, but it's all procedural at this point, and in a death penalty case procedural takes time."

"Death penalty. On accountability? Isn't that a hard stretch under Illinois Supreme Court rulings?"

"Three young men gunned down very much in cold blood, very much in broad daylight. You know how much the court of public opinion can sway a judge and jury, despite precedent."

"Glad I don't have your job, Bruce."

"An astute observation, young lady. Now, I have to meet with those two other attorneys. Talk to Tina. It'll probably be at least two weeks, maybe a month before this all gets in motion, but I'll need you ready to go."

"Understood, sir."

I clicked my heels together, bowed my head slightly, and about-faced. A bit of military decorum was my way of showing Bruce respect. I hoped I was in the kind of shape he was in at seventy-four. We'd talked running a couple of times. He was never one to enter events unless they were for a charity, and he'd stopped running events years ago. He still ran thirteen miles every Sunday, though, and a few miles two mornings during the week. He was slow, but he was still doing it.

***

Ronald's condo in Hoffman was among the many non-descript newer developments covering much of the western suburbs. If not for the numbers on the units and personal decorations in or around windows, one unit looked almost identical to the next. Ronald's unit was typical for a male of his age: I could see no unique or identifying features from outside. Foot traffic was mostly moms with their children. It was the middle of the afternoon on a sunny day with low humidity. School would be getting out soon though, and I imagined the neighborhood would get much noisier.

I rang the doorbell and waited. I noticed a little statuette on the window sill, some kind of wizard or something. Probably supposed to protect Ronald's place. It was intricately carved and made me curious about its origin. I grabbed it, and for a moment my breath hitched and my eyes closed. Maybe I did need to cut back on my smoking.

A couple minutes later, I rang the bell again, waiting only a minute before knocking on the door. I didn't hear any movement from inside, see shades moving, or see shadows crossing anywhere. Ronald wasn't home. I'd check back later.

Back in my Rav, I grabbed the file and read through it again. There was really nowhere else to go at the moment. I would have to wait to see if Diana was able to find out anything from visiting his employer. I grabbed the other file with the serves. One was in Schaumburg, the other in Palatine. Serving a wage garnishment was simple work. Payroll departments were accustomed to them; it was a process, not an event. An order from the court directing them to deduct money from someone's wages, the wage garnishment gave them a prescribed formula for determining how much to deduct. It didn't cost the company anything and took all of fifteen minutes to put in place in automated payroll systems. Except at small companies where people knew each other, a wage garnishment action was as notable as a memo about a change in company policy regarding acceptable clothes on casual Friday. Serving them would probably kill an hour and a half, maybe two. That would put me back at Ronald's around dinner time for most people.

I was on my way back to Ronald's when Diana called.

"Hello, Diana. How did it go?"

"Hi, Sam. About half and half. None of his coworkers had trouble talking to the chica looking for him. How'd it go there?"

"Garnishments served, no sign of Ronald, but I'm almost back to check again. What did they say?"

"That's the not so good part. They were all sayin' that he was actin' all weird and angry...actin' like he had a short fuse, an' I, ya know, played along that was not like him. One dude said he hadn't shown up for their poker game for three weeks, and he was one of the regulars."

"Huh. Okay, I'm going to check back here, maybe sit on it for a while. See if there's any real movement or if he's just got burglar lights programmed. If I get nothing, we'll pick it back up tomorrow after we get those other four serves completed. You want to go north or south?"

I heard the sound of papers being shuffled. "Well, since you givin' me the choice, boss-lady, guess I'll go see how the other half lives."

"Okay, you want Lake Forest, you got it. Just remember: pinky finger if you stop to eat."

Diana chuckled. "One must be civilized, of course."

"Should I bring you back some food? Serves are in the burbs, but I could make a quick diversion to Halsted. Rib tips and greens?"

"Sounds good, Sam," Diana said, pausing. "You know, it's never too late to learn to cook like your mom does."

I had to stop myself from responding too quickly. "Well, when you see me bring in some knitting needles, we can start a recipe swap in the building."

"Cute, boss-lady."

"Diana, if I started cooking I'd steal your thunder. You got almost everyone in the building buying empanadillas from you, and Jamie calls you his tostones queen."

"He's smart."

"Not sure how you do it. I mean, when you were working at the club and bringing them in it made sense, kind of hand in hand. Okay, my little chica, I'm here. I'll be here until around seven, and then I'll head to the office and grab the serves for tomorrow. We good on the backgrounds?"

"We will be 'fore I leave."

"Okay. Have a good night. See you tomorrow afternoon."

As I pulled up in front of Ronald's building, I tried to push away the thoughts that Diana's comment had brought rushing forward. I was never going to be, nor did I particularly desire to become, a domestic queen. At the same time, I couldn't deny those recipes were part of my heritage.

Why couldn't I have inherited some of your musical talent?

I closed my eyes, tilted my head back, and let out a muffled growl. I reached for the pack of cigarettes that sat on the passenger seat, my mind back to the movements around the building. I could see people going in and out of the second story units. I pressed the button to lower my window and lit my cigarette.

As the smoke drifted out, the smell of barbecue drifted in. I wondered about my mom. She was down in Machu Picchu, some kind of mecca for people on their spiritual journey, and I was almost certain she was paying little attention to her doctor's advice. As I watched my reflection in the rearview mirror, smoke drifting out of my mouth toward the open window, the irony was obvious.

***

As I walked down the hallway to the office, my mind worked on what direction to take to find Ronald. The thought he might be dead had invaded a part of my brain overnight. I hadn't spoken with Kathy yet, and she'd been out of town for two days on a business trip. I would have liked to interrupt her with good news. She would be back in town tonight on a late flight, and I hoped I would have something for her before her plane touched down.

I opened the door and was not surprised to see Diana seated, going over an order sheet. "Djou in for empanadillas, Sam?"

"Straight trade? Got your rib tips and greens in the bag."

"Hmm...that'll get you eight empanadillas, but I know you always get some for Dre too."

"Take care of my teacher...well, actually it's his wife that likes them."

"Happy wife, happy life."

I grinned. "Really? Maybe we should do a few infidelity cases. See if you still hang with that little nutshell."

"Oooh, so sensitive."

I narrowed my eyes at her. "No calls from you, so I'm guessing the serves both went straight and simple. Your affidavits notarized yet?"

"Not yet."

"Okay, if you don't mind," I said, placing the bag of food down on her desk. I pulled the affidavits from the earlier serves out of my notebook and handed them to Diana. "Can you run downstairs and get them all notarized? Of course, after you're done conducting other business on my time."

I smiled broadly, and Diana smiled back, her middle finger scratching her nose as she looked up at me.

"Djou know, boss-lady, sometimes I think maybe you shoulda went into stand-up."

I blew her a kiss. "My little chica, what would I do without your support?"

"Right, I'm sayin'."

"Okay, okay, enough playtime...I'm thinking we might need to do a little more direct digging on the internet with respect to Ronald. When you get back with the affidavits, come in and let's see if we can brainstorm something."

It was Diana's idea to go straight to searching the Florida local newspapers for his name. A quick search revealed that the two towns with addresses for him were both served by the same three papers. Diana sat with me as we searched. When the computer kicked back an item from six weeks ago, we both read it silently.

"Damn, Sam."

"Yeah," I said, not nearly as surprised as Diana sounded.

According to the obituary, Ronald passed due to complications of a long-standing medical condition. It listed where a memorial service would be held and stated that, per Ronald's wishes, his ashes would be scattered in the ocean, returning to where life began. The memorial service had been held a day before Kathy hired me to find Ronald. We both read it over a few times, trying to reconcile what we were reading with Kathy's concern. How could she not know?

"Sam, you got to let her get home before you tell her."

"Yeah, not something to tell her when she's in motion. Damn. I'm trying to imagine how her ex didn't tell her."

"It must have been really ugly between them. That's cold. Never seen somethin' that cold."

"All right," I said, pulling my thoughts together. "Let's print it out. I'll see if I can get a hold of Kathy."

Diana stared at me. "Sam, you're not going to tell her over the phone, are you?"

"No. I'll meet her at her house when she gets back. She said she'd be home around 9:30."

“Okay...okay. For a minute, it sounded like you were just going to call her with the news. That would be cruel.”

“Right. Even I’m not that cold.”

***

I debated whether or not to call Kathy with a harmless pretext for coming out to meet with her so that she wouldn’t be caught off guard completely. I decided a text would be better. I wouldn’t be taking a chance of talking to her and letting it get too far. Knowing how important this was to her, I calculated she wouldn’t think too much if I simply texted her that I’d like to meet to talk about the search status.

Standing in her driveway, looking up at the bright, almost full moon, I wondered about its effect on people. Between the military and this line of work, I knew it was definitely true that some people were more subject to the changes in atmospheric pressure that it caused. I took a long draw on my cigarette and realized it was the third one I’d smoked in the last half-hour.

I’d seen some of what I thought was the worst in relationships growing up. I’d seen my mother taken advantage of by men who were supposed to be her managers, seen her take abuse, and seen her persist in looking for some kind of serious relationship. But Kathy's ex neglecting to inform her of their son's death was probably the worst indictment of marriage I'd seen. I wasn't sure how exactly I was going to tell Kathy. I was certain I wanted to get her in the house before we started talking, but I was also certain her first words after hello would be Have you found him, Sam? Have you spoken with him? Is he all right?

I wasn't a mother, and it was impossible to imagine the kind of deep hurt this was going to cause her. Diana still grieved occasionally for the baby she lost to miscarriage, even taking time each year for a little memorial service. I knew other parents whose entire lives seemed wrapped around their children. What I had seen growing up and from doing this kind of work also made me aware of parents who were anything but attentive. In this moment, knowing Kathy was one of the former, I wasn't comfortable with my role in this.

I looked at my watch. There was enough time for another cigarette, and I walked over to my Rav, reaching in for my coffee as well.

"Caffeine and nicotine, the wonder drugs," I said aloud.

I was halfway through the cigarette when I saw headlight beams splash across the wide driveway. Kathy's house was on two wooded acres, so it was a few moments before the livery vehicle approached. I put the cigarette out, flicking the butt into the garbage can off the side of the driveway. I breathed in and out deeply; this was not going to be easy.

"Sam, thank you for coming out tonight," Kathy said, rushing toward me, holding her garment bag over her shoulder, a brown leather computer bag in her other hand. "I really appreciate it."

"Let me help you," I said, reaching for the garment bag. She dug for her keys in her pocket as she walked, and I was glad for the preoccupation. I wanted her inside when we talked.

As we approached the door, the motion-activated light came on, and Kathy put the laptop bag down, picking the right key and opening the door before she picked the bag up. She held the door for me, and I leaned my back into it, allowing her to step in first. The kitchen light came on, and then one in the small living room.

"Grab a seat, Sam. I'm going to check on Geronimo before we talk. You can put on coffee or water for tea if you like." Geronimo was her cat.

I debated about coffee or tea. I was fairly certain Kathy would opt for tea, so I took the kettle off the stove, filled it, and put it on to heat up. I looked around the kitchen, closing my eyes and sighing more than once at the pictures on the fridge.

"Now," Kathy said, stepping back into the living room that was crowded with her wood sculptures and two oversized recliners. She held a purring Geronimo on one arm, petting her with the other hand. "Tell me how's it going with finding Ronald?"

"Kathy," I said, stepping closer to her. "I really think you should sit down."

"Oh, God. No, Sam. No," Kathy said, her eyes closed, her mouth open.

I caught her arm as her knees buckled, shifting to her side and helping her to sit down. I didn't have to say anything more. I stood there, one hand on her shoulder, the other instinctively on her arm; then, I crouched down, reaching an arm across her shoulders, allowing her to let her head rest on my shoulder. Her tears flowed freely, broken occasionally by a gulping inhalation. I didn't know how long it would be before she would be able to ask questions, but I'd let her take whatever time she needed.

***

I eyed the glass before picking it up. Part of me knew I should leave it on the bar, politely excuse myself, and walk home. That part didn't win the fight. I picked it up, emptied the rest of the drink, put it back on the bar top, and nodded to Niko to refill it. I was never a sloppy drunk, so I knew Niko would oblige.

"C'mon, Sam, I know that agitated pensiveness. Holding onto it isn't going to help."

"I don't know, Becca," I replied, looking away from Rebecca and then back into her eyes. Whatever had happened that night with Stephanie seemed to have intensified my emotions, and I wasn't fighting them.

Rebecca returned my stare, which said a lot. We had shared some hard truths, from her mistakes the day she was shot to, finally, my mistake with Jacky, but I wasn't sure if I wanted to talk to her about what had happened with Kathy or where my thoughts were going from there. She was reading me the same way I read people, and maybe she was right.

"Well, this is different, but it's part of it too. Sam I Am's getting married and bringing his Greek wife back."

Becca sat back and dropped her hands to her lap. "I'm sorry, Sam. Really I am. But the way you kept saying he wanted more, you had to know that day was going to come."

I couldn't tell if it was an I told you so thing or if she was just waiting for a greater reaction from me. I couldn't say anything really. Just a month or two before leaving for Greece, Sam had told me about wanting someone who was more a part of his life. Had I ignored a hint he was dropping about the unusually long trip? He had asked me to go with but didn't try to convince me when I said I couldn't take the time, didn't offer to have me come for part of it. Becca had told me the next day she thought Sam may have taken my saying no as a signal I wasn't going to be what he wanted.

"True, but it's all weird...the timing with Jacky and everything," I lied again, hoping she would let it go. I wasn't going to tell her about the night with Stephanie down in Tennessee or the song I was still struggling with. It was a lot, and I didn't want it coming out sideways.

"Sam, what's underneath it all? I know you; there's something more."

"Okay, okay, Becca. You want to know about my agitated pensiveness?"

Her eyes narrowed, and she sat up in her chair, clearly a bit more interested, anxious, like she was waiting to see what would happen next. She seemed a little surprised too, maybe because my calm, collected self wasn't present.

"Here's what I got to share today, what I got to see as the culmination of a beautiful, loving relationship that led to marriage. Two people are so in love they get married, right? Then they express their love so deeply they have a kid, right?"

I reached over and took another sip of tequila. "But things happen and they grow apart...and ain't that a cute fucking euphemism? So, they grow apart and divorce and go through all that angry shit. Time passes, and mom can't reach her son who's now twenty-four. So, what does she do? She calls her friend's daughter, the private detective, to find him, right? That's what you do, right? Anything for your kids."

"Okay," Rebecca responded, a questioning look on her face. She sat back in her chair again, this time her eyes slightly widened, one hand reaching up to her chin, index finger across her bottom lip.

"So, I do my best, right? I do my best to find her son; she's my mom's friend. I do my best, and I find him. You know where I find him? I find him dead. Dead six weeks before mom started missing him. Cremated three weeks before mom called me. Memorial service that weekend."

"Jesus, Sam."

"Yes, Jesus H. fucking Christ, Becca. Her fucking ex-husband never even called to tell her. I had to go to her house and tell her. I had to look her worry, her concern, her undying maternal love in the eye and say, oh, sorry he's fucking dead. Love is a many splendored fucking thing, right?"

"Sam, maybe you should…"

"No, no Becca, not yet," I answered, feeling the alcohol-induced emotion growing. I didn't want to hurt her, but I'd opened the floodgates. Now, I was struggling to rein it in. "Relationships, shit. Before my mom left, we had quite the discussion. She was asking about why I'm not settling down, asking about why I won't talk about my father and other stuff—pushing me hard to go places I didn't want to go. Talking to me about what I need to believe in."

"Moms do that; sometimes I do that."

"I understand that, but that's different, Becca. She's still pushing, still thinking she can make me into someone else at forty-four."

"Maybe. Maybe she just wants more for you."

"More for me? Like what Kathy had? Like what all the people who want to hire me for infidelity investigations have? Put my time and faith in that? Yeah, I want some of that shit! What if I'm not looking for the more she wants me to have? What if I'm good where I'm at?"

"I don't know, Sam...are you?"

I glared at her. I had to let that go. I could feel the anger rising, and it wanted release. Niko left to go downstairs and help with the closing. He left the bottle of anejo near our shot glasses. Rebecca was still slowly sipping her second, and I saw her slide the bottle closer to her.

"Then she hits me with her my people shit. My fucking people. My fucking people that left a little girl, eight years old, lying on the playground at recess, bleeding and bruised from a beating cuz she wasn't black enough. Knocked her around in the neighborhood cause her skin color was too light—adults sittin' on the porch not doin' a damn thing to stop it. Believing in that shit going to save me and the world?"

I took another sip. "Believe in making the system work for me, right? Join the Army, go to law school, right? Rich white men either grabbin' my ass or riggin' the system against me cause I'm not really part of the club. Believe in our country that's bombin' the shit out of civilians all over the world for oil and strategic fucking interests and our justice system that's plain criminal? My father was another white asshole skipped out on my mom, wasn't there for me, but damn if he was the only motha fucka pullin' that shit. She talks about me believing in something more. Bullshit! She pulled up all my shit, Becca, and then hit me with more."

"Sam," Becca reached across the bar top to my arm. I didn't pull my arm away, but I couldn't look at her. I took a more measured sip from the shot glass.

"Damnit, I was raped by a righteous, reverend man of god, Rebecca! Raped in the house of the Lord! But she want me to find my spirituality, put my time and faith into that. I was thirteen, scared, hurt, felt like I was evil, like I did something wrong! Watched as people came forward to keep the 'event' secret as much as to help me. People do that shit, still do it today. Yeah, religions have made the world a better place, right?"

"Oh my God."

"Yep." I took another drink from the shot glass and saw my hand shaking. It was coming out ugly and I had to try pulling it back. Becca knew me better than almost anyone else in my life, but I could read the impact of my words on her face: she was learning there was much about me she still didn't know.

"Don't nobody just keep it real. Shit, you been abused? Get in line, motherfucker."

"Damn, Sam." Rebecca slid off her stool. She looked straight into my eyes. She knew, and she waited.

I took in a deep breath. "Mama and her spiritual friends...fucking meditate and see the good, find the fucking balance. Machu motha fuckin' Picchu."

I gulped down the rest of the shot and slammed the glass down on the bar. It hit at an angle and with enough force to shatter in my hands, a jagged piece piercing the web of flesh between my thumb and forefinger. I stared at it for a second.

"Sam, don't!"

I pulled it out, knowing there were no arteries or major blood vessels there. I held the piece of glass for a moment, staring at it.

"Motherfucker," I said quietly.

"Sam?"

I could feel a single tear rolling down my left cheek, but I wasn't ready for Rebecca's hug. I tossed the shard of glass into the garbage can behind the bar, picking up a napkin and holding the hand straight up to control the blood flow.

"So you see, Becca," I said, my voice calm, the emotion rolling back down. "It's a lot, a lot going on that shouldn't be, a lot going on that makes life more difficult and isn't really necessary. World is too fucked-up, complicated by everybody trying to put everyone and everything into their own little trick bags. Your boys, you know, they're cute as hell. But damn if I want to bring kids into a world so...just plain fucked up."

Rebecca held her arms out. I stood still for a moment, and then took a step forward, stutter-stepping and almost tripping. I wrapped my arms tightly around her, burying my face in her shoulder. I could feel my teeth grinding and tears being squeezed out of eyes that wouldn't open. I didn't know how long I stood there, but when my eyes finally opened, they burned.

"Thanks, Becca," I said and stepped back. "Thank you for letting me have that moment."

"You ever think maybe of trying to talk to a counselor some more?"

"I've talked to a few counselors over time...talked enough."

"Okay, Sam. You going to have someone look at that?"

"I looked at it. I've seen you looking at it. Band aid and a little being careful for a couple days is all it needs. Can you do me a favor? Do the rest of closing?"

Rebecca looked at me for a moment, her face going through changes. "Jesus, Sam. Yes, I'll do the rest of the closing. Get some sleep...take a day to do nothing."

"Remember," I answered jokingly, knowing she was a fan of Peaceful Warrior, the movie my mother had pushed on me a few years back. "There's never nothing going on."

She smiled. I smiled back, executed a proper about face, and walked out the back way. Monday wasn't far away, and Rebecca was right about one thing: I did need some rest and down time, even if I no longer knew what that really looked like. As I let the door to the club close, I looked at my two bandaged hands. I thought for a moment about what Stephanie had said, something about my anger wanting to fight to keep hold, or something like that. She was definitely right. Whatever had happened in Tennessee, and even with understanding a little better about my mother, that anger didn't let go.

I took out and lit a cigarette, wiped a tear from the corner of my eye, and looked up at the full moon.

"Straight up bitch...comma optional," I joked lamely and started my slow walk home.

***

I wasn't sure who thought something was so important they needed to call every ten minutes, but I was certain the headache pulling tightly on my brain and twisting would speak clearly to whoever it was. I didn't have any investigations that were awaiting a dramatic conclusion, and if anything serious had happened at the club, Rebecca would have been at my door, not calling.

I sat up, grabbing the phone off the nightstand. There were too many voicemails. I saw Bruce's number first, so I went to that voicemail. It wasn't urgent, just Tina telling me the judge had granted the motion for special appointment, so barring any motion from the State's Attorney, I would be a court-appointed special investigator on behalf of Damion Jackson. I knew that would mean something to other people, but at the moment, I wasn't feeling particularly moved.

I reached over to the nightstand, grabbing the pack of cigarettes and lighter. Was there coffee in the pot? I walked slowly to the kitchen. Yes, there was almost a half pot of coffee. I poured a cup, putting it in the microwave for fifty seconds. I leaned back against the counter, one hand holding onto the granite to steady myself, the other reaching for the cigarettes and lighter. When the microwave beeped, I punched the door button, wanting the sound to cease immediately.

Coffee and cigarette in one hand, I picked up the phone and walked over to the glass and chrome coffee table in the living room. Dropping into the oversized, black leather arm chair, I closed my eyes and dragged. I let the smoke escape slowly, sitting up slowly as it did. There was no changing what had happened last night, but I owed my mom and Becca an apology, not for what I'd said, but for how I'd said it. I needed to be direct with my mom, not angry. She didn't have to like my life, but she needed to accept it, and neither of us was helping that process along.

The phone rang again, and I almost knocked over my coffee grabbing it to stop the sound. I looked at the display, and my headache disappeared in the sudden sound of blood rushing in my ears. It was Gladys.

"Gladys," I said, my voice rough. "I don't mean you any disrespect, but just tell me straight, no drama."

"Oh, Sam...Sam, I know you keep your—"

"Gladys, is my mother okay?"

My voice vibrated through my head, harsh and clipped, but I wasn't interested in a life lesson from Gladys.

"I'm so sorry, Sam. She's gone."